"It's snowing," she said in amazement.

Some of the worry eased from his face and he smiled. Ella couldn't get over the feeling that she recognized that smile from...somewhere.

"It is," Kyle said in agreement.

"I can't remember the last time I've seen it snow. It must have been..." The memory disappeared and she closed her eyes trying to recapture it. In her heart she knew it was real and important, but it was gone.

"What do you remember?" he asked.

Her face creased into a frown. "I don't know."

"It's getting colder out. Let's get you warm."

They were halfway to the ▒▒▒▒ the sound of tires squealing close ▒▒▒▒ ▒▒ttention. A nondescript bei▒▒ ▒▒ ▒t windows charged throug▒ ▒▒ ▒ght for them.

"Run!" he ▒▒▒▒ ▒▒ hand, all but hauling her alon▒ ▒▒▒▒cle. They'd just reached the cove▒ ▒▒ ▒he occupants of the car opened fire.

Mary Alford was inspired to become a writer after reading romantic suspense greats Victoria Holt and Phyllis Whitney. Soon, creating characters and throwing them into dangerous situations that test their faith came naturally for Mary. In 2012 Mary entered the Speed Dating contest hosted by Love Inspired Suspense and later received "the call." Writing for Love Inspired Suspense has been a dream come true for Mary.

Books by Mary Alford

Love Inspired Suspense

Forgotten Past
Rocky Mountain Pursuit
Deadly Memories

DEADLY MEMORIES

MARY ALFORD

HARLEQUIN® LOVE INSPIRED® SUSPENSE

Recycling programs
for this product may
not exist in your area.

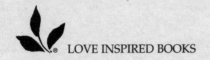 LOVE INSPIRED BOOKS

ISBN-13: 978-0-373-45715-1

Deadly Memories

www.Harlequin.com

Printed in U.S.A.

Peace I leave with you, my peace I give unto you:
not as the world giveth, give I unto you.
Let not your heart be troubled, neither let it be afraid.
–John 14:27

To the men and women who stand on the front lines of our freedom and face down the enemy every day. Thank you for your service.

ONE

They were coming. She could hear them arguing as they neared. After all these years, they still didn't have a clue she spoke fluent Dari.

Ella listened closely. The reality of what they said threatened to crush her. It was the last thing she expected. They were planning to kill her.

What had changed in the past twenty-four hours? Alhasan's orders had been clear yesterday. The men were to escort her to the location. She was being transported to the United States. She had a job to do. As long as she did it, he would let her live…along with the child.

The American. He'd visited her prison cell a handful of times, and in spite of Alhasan's bragging, Ella believed he was the real person in charge. He'd spoken like someone who wielded a lot of power when he'd made it clear to Alhasan that he didn't believe she would follow through with her orders in spite of Alhasan's assurances.

If he'd ordered her death, where did that leave Joseph? She couldn't think about what might happen to the child and not go crazy, and she couldn't lose it. Joseph's life depended on it.

For most of the day, she'd heard them moving things

from the prison. She hadn't seen Alhasan or Joseph again and her fear for the boy's safety mushroomed.

Now, as the young men grew near, a new uneasiness boiled in her gut. Their conversation had become increasingly agitated. Someone was coming. They were in a rush to leave. Tying up loose ends. One of Alhasan's young flunkies had decided she wasn't worth risking his life to save hers.

Immediately Ella's fighting instinct kicked in. She wasn't about to die here in this cell. Not after all she'd given up to *him*. She needed help. God's help.

Please give me strength, she prayed with all her heart as the key slipped into the lock and the door to her cell flew open, slamming angrily against the stone wall.

"On your feet." One of the young men shouted the order at her.

Ella's heart slammed against her chest. She slowly rose to a sitting position; the effort left her struggling for breath. Despair was close and she clamped down hard on her bottom lip until she tasted blood. She wouldn't show weakness in front of them. Wouldn't beg for mercy. She'd go out fighting for Joseph and for herself.

The yelling one moved closer. He had a knife in his hand. They were both so young. Barely teenagers and clearly new to Alhasan's cause.

"I said on your feet," he snapped as if trying to rally his confidence. He grabbed her arm and yanked her to her feet. A tidal wave of pain tore through her. She slumped against her captor, unable to stand on her own.

Her weakness took him by surprise. He shoved her away. "Turn around," he demanded while slapping the knife against his leg. She was pretty certain neither of them had killed before. They didn't have the look of hardened killers.

Concentrate!

She struggled to clear her jumbled thoughts. She would have only seconds to disarm them both and run for her life. Otherwise...

"Did you hear something?" the teenager standing guard asked in an uneasy tone. His partner didn't respond. "I'll check it out. You take care of her."

Left alone, the young man grew increasingly anxious. "I said turn around."

Ella slowly faced the wall, her pulse hammering in her ears. He moved closer. This was it. Her whole existence came down to just a handful of seconds.

He grabbed her and pulled her close. She slumped against him once more. This time it was all part of the ruse. She suppressed the revulsion she felt at being near him. She wanted him to think she was too fragile to fight back.

He raised the knife. With a final prayer for strength speeding through her head, Ella grabbed the hand holding the weapon. Surprised, the young man hesitated for a beat. It was all she needed.

Before he realized what she'd done, Ella twisted his arm behind his back. He yelped in pain as she squeezed his arm with all her remaining strength until the knife flew from his hand.

Acting on an instinct she didn't know she possessed but could only believe came straight from God, Ella wrapped her arm tight around his throat and choked him. With every second ticking by feeling like an eternity, the young man finally lost consciousness and slipped to the floor at her feet.

Ella grabbed the knife and stumbled for the door. The effort of disarming her captor had greatly depleted her small amount of strength. Leaning against the door frame for support, she sucked in air. She had to find Joseph and keep moving. She had to get them both out of here before the partner came back. Because they would eventually kill her for failing Alhasan's mission. Her gut instinct told her she couldn't do what he wanted. She wasn't the killer he'd tried to convince her she was.

Slipping from the cell, Ella eased along the dank, foul-swelling hallway that oozed water. Nothing more than a single lightbulb kept the darkness at bay.

She headed toward the right at a frantic pace, all the while hoping she wasn't walking straight into the enemy's arms. This was a part of the prison she'd never seen. On the rare occasions she'd been allowed to shower, her captors had insisted she wear a blindfold. Still, her sense of direction was keen. She was positive they'd taken her down the hallway and deeper into the depth of the prison.

The hall was lined with doors containing what appeared to be more than half a dozen cells just like hers. Was Joseph in one of them? Would she find him alive? Her stomach clenched at what those two young men might have done.

She tried the first door. It swung open freely and she stepped inside. Within the cell's dark bowels she could see a crumpled mass on the floor. Joseph! She raced toward it and found the lifeless body of a man. It wasn't Joseph. Relief rushed over her and threatened to buckle her knees.

Slowly, she knelt next to the man. He'd been dead long enough for rigor mortis to come and go. A single gunshot to his head.

Ella touched his shoulder. "I'm sorry." She could only imagine what he'd gone through during those final moments before death.

A quick check of the rest of the cells proved they were empty as well, and her concern for Joseph's safety intensified. Had Alhasan taken the boy with him to ensure her cooperation? She'd hold on to the hope that he would keep his word and she'd find a way to save Joseph.

With every move making it harder to breathe, Ella continued slowly down the hall while holding the wall for support. In her best estimate, the man she'd disarmed should be waking in a matter of minutes. Where was the second man? Time was critical. If they captured her again, she'd be dead.

The hall took an immediate ninety-degree left turn. Ella flattened against the wall and eased along until she could see the next passage. On her right was what looked like a rudimentary office. She slowly advanced toward it. Windows! They reflected a night sky filled with stars. She hadn't seen stars or the moon or felt the sun against her skin in so long.

As she moved cautiously toward the exit, her legs were so weak she wasn't sure how far they would carry her. Her hands weren't much better. They shook with such tremors that it took several tries before the door opened in her hand. Alhasan had ensured that she had just enough food to keep her alive. But not enough for the possibility that she'd be strong enough to escape. What he hadn't counted on as her uncrushable will to live.

She stepped through it feeling like a child on Christmas morning.

Ella glanced back at the prison that had been her home for more years than she remembered. She'd suffered greatly here. She'd barely been alive when she'd first arrived. The head injury she'd sustained when captured was so severe that she'd been in and out of consciousness for weeks after she'd arrived. When she'd woken up, she was in her prison cell, her memory gone. She hadn't even known her name. The scar across her face and the one that parted her hair were permanent reminders of how close to death she'd come.

Ella was positive she wouldn't have survived if it were not for the gentle care she'd received from the woman who'd shared her cell. She'd been barely hanging on to life, yet she recalled the woman talking to her about God. Praying for her. Singing soothing songs.

But her memory of how the woman had looked was fuzzy. Sometimes, if she closed her eyes, Ella could almost remember the woman's face. She'd looked much like herself—or maybe it was just her memory playing tricks.

What she could recall with clarity was the day Alhasan took the woman away. After that, Ella never saw her again. She wasn't sure how long it was before Alhasan brought her Joseph. Weeks. Months, even.

Her love for Joseph soon became the only thing that kept her going through the years. Leaving the prison without him now felt like she was deserting him. She didn't know what to do. The thought of such an innocent child subject to Alhasan's cruelty ripped her heart out. But she'd searched the cells. Joseph wasn't there.

She would have to survive long enough to find him. To do that she had to keep moving. Put space between herself and the prison.

Ella dug out her necklace from where she'd hidden it years ago inside the small pocket of her jeans. Each time they'd given her new clothes, she'd carefully hid the chain in the same pocket while terrified that Alhasan or one of his men would find it. Always surprised when they hadn't.

A simple silver ring with two entwined hearts dangled from the chain. She couldn't remember where it came from, but through the years she found a small comfort in knowing it belonged to another lifetime. A happier time. Ella put the necklace on for the first time and started walking.

The simple act quickly took its toll on her weak body, forcing frequent breaks just to catch her breath. After she'd covered some distance, she took stock of her surroundings. All around was desert. To her left, mountains loomed against the night sky.

Where was she? Like she'd done endless times, she tried to recall the slightest memory of being captured, but it was useless.

Fighting back the hopelessness, she headed for the mountain range. At least they would provide some cover. She could watch the prison and surrounding area safely from there. Her gut told her Joseph was still nearby. She wouldn't leave until she found him or she died trying.

That she'd escaped at all was a blessing. She would do everything in her power to save Joseph, and she'd leave the rest of it in God's hands.

Ella had barely covered a quarter of a mile when something unsettling caught her attention. The ground beneath her feet rumbled with the sound of an approaching vehicle. She could see its lights. There wasn't as much as a bush to hide behind. She was in the open and exposed. What if it was Alhasan? The thought threatened to take away what little bit of courage she possessed.

She was still standing, frozen in terror, when a Humvee came to a screaming halt in front of her.

The driver jumped from the vehicle with his weapon drawn. "Get your hands in the air," he shouted.

His voice…his voice. She recognized it!

Ella sucked in a shocked breath, imprisoned by the intimate sound. Had she heard correctly? Maybe she was delusional and this was all part of a dream?

Fragmented recollections flew through her head. No, she was positive she knew his voice. She struggled to hold her focus.

"I said get your hands in the air," he ordered once more. Ella hesitated for a second longer then lifted her hands, the knife she'd taken from the camp soldier still in her left hand.

This new threat quickly spotted, his tone turned deadly. "Drop the weapon. Now."

She hurriedly let it go. The man moved closer and kicked the knife out of her reach.

"Get down on your knees and put your hands behind your head," he demanded while keeping his weapon trained securely on her head.

The faintest of memories teased her briefly then disappeared. How did she know him?

She silently prayed for the strength to do as he asked. Ella dropped awkwardly to her knees. Bile rose in her throat and she swayed back and forth, fighting to stay conscious.

She squinted through the headlights. If she could just make out his face…

The man shifted on his feet, and then she knew. With a mixture of shock and horror, her suspicions were confirmed. She definitely recognized him. She'd seen his face dozens of times in the photos Alhasan had shown her. This was the leader of the elite CIA team known as the Scorpions.

She'd seen photos for each of the team's eight members. Alhasan had told her that Kyle Jennings had created the Scorpions after the war to fight the rising number of terrorist groups in Afghanistan and in an effort to prevent weapons from falling into the wrong hands. He'd raged on about the Scorpions' interference in his activities and bragged about taking out key members in the past. Then he'd laid out what was expected of her if she wanted to save Joseph.

"I can't believe it's you," she whispered in total disbelief, still not certain she wasn't hallucinating.

This was the Scorpions' leader. The man she was supposed to kill.

Somehow, Agent Kyle Jennings managed to hang on to his composure. Even weak and raspy, when she'd spoken she'd sounded exactly like…Lena. The thought struck home like a lightning bolt and he immediately rejected the notion.

Impossible. He'd buried his wife almost seven years ago when her badly burned body was discovered in the desert close to this same area. The overwhelming grief and heartache he still experienced every time he thought about losing her assured him there was no coming back from that. Lena was gone. And he had a purpose to fulfill.

He'd come here to meet Hadir after receiving an ominous text message from his asset. *She* was unexpected. What was she doing out here anyway, in the middle of a territory the military had nicknamed *no-man's-land* for good reason? This Afghanistan desert terrain was under the control of the Fox, the CIA's most wanted terrorist target.

Kyle recalled something disturbing Hadir had told him recently. The man had said the Fox had bragged about grooming a female operative for a critical mission that would shock the world.

And he was certain this woman recognized him. The only question was how? Because of the criticalness of their missions, anonymity was key. The Scorpion team members' names and personal information were closely guarded. There were no pictures of the team in circulation. Their background files were kept in a safe at Scorpion headquarters in Painted Rock Valley, Colorado.

How would she know him?

With the lights at his back, he moved a little to the left so that he could see the woman's face more clearly. Through the dust motes caught in the headlights, what he saw just about took his legs out from underneath him. She *looked* like Lena. Her hair—raven black—was the same color as Lena's, although it was much longer and looked as if it hadn't been cared for properly in a while.

But it was her eyes that really got to him. They were dark brown and soulful, like his wife's had been.

His mouth twisted involuntarily at a memory. He recalled how he used to joke with Lena that at times it was as if she could look right through him. He saw the same expression in this woman's gaze and it was gut-wrenching. Shocking.

He crushed the tiniest bit of hope taking life inside his heart. He couldn't go there.

Kyle struggled to pull his thoughts together. "You recognize me?" The question came out sharper than

he intended, mostly because everything about her un-
nerved him.

He waited for an answer she clearly had no intention
of giving. She shook her head and stared at the ground.

Frustrated, Kyle glanced around the area. It was just
the two of them, but clearly she believed she recognized
him.

I can't believe it's you.

It didn't sit well. Had she escaped from somewhere
or was she part of a trap set by the notorious Fox? Her
appearance certainly seemed to confirm someone who
had been imprisoned. She was disheveled, her clothes
tattered. Still, he didn't like the fact that she'd appeared
out of nowhere.

"Answer the question. How do you know me?" he
barked, and she flinched as if he'd struck her. Kyle didn't
let up. He had to know. "What's your name? Why are
you out here alone?"

She closed her eyes. She appeared so frail—barely
hanging on—so unlike his strong, confident wife.

Until he knew her true identity and why she was wandering the desert, he had to treat her as a hostile.

She swallowed visibly. "My name?" she managed, as
if confused.

"Yes, your name." Kyle didn't try to hide his annoy-
ance. She was fading fast and he needed answers.

"It's…Ella…Weiss." She didn't sound very positive.
"Please, you have to let me go. I have to find him." Help-
less tears filled her eyes. He watched her clench her hands
into fists until the tears disappeared.

"Who do you have to find?" he asked, even more
concerned. What was she doing out here alone? Who
was she searching for?

She moaned softly, and it captured his full attention. He was losing her. Kyle rushed to her side. He wasn't in time to catch her before she slipped to the desert surface.

He knelt next to her and felt for a pulse. It was there but weak. She had a scar that ran the length of her right cheek and another far more severe one that parted her hair. Someone had hurt her badly. He couldn't imagine the pain she'd suffered. He turned her hands up and swallowed back anger. Her fingerprints had been deliberately burned off. They didn't want her identified.

He couldn't stop his thoughts from wandering back to Lena. He'd known the moment he met her that he wanted to spend the rest of his life with her. They'd dated only a year before he'd asked her to marry him. Their five-year marriage had still been in the honeymoon stage when she'd disappeared. He shivered as recalled the horrible night he'd learned of Lena's death.

Because of the effects of the fire, her body had been unidentifiable except for the wedding ring still on her left hand. The inscription "To the love of my life" was on the inside of the band. There had been no mistaking the ring he'd given his wife on the day they'd wed. But knowing she'd been wearing it was the most confusing part.

Lena had never worn her wedding ring on a mission before. As a seasoned operative, she knew better than to wear anything that might jeopardize her cover story. When he'd seen the band, he'd been shocked. It was a rookie mistake and one he was sure Lena never would have made. But then again, she hadn't been herself in the days before she left for the mission. Something had been wrong, and yet she'd refused to talk to him about it.

Now, the similarities between his wife's death and this woman left him unsettled. They'd both been found in the same area, and someone had gone to great lengths to keep their identities a secret.

Something around the woman's neck caught his attention as it glistened in the headlights. A necklace. He lifted the chain in his hand. A small silver ring caught the light.

"What's happening out there, Kyle?" He barely registered Sam Lansford's voice coming through his radio. He couldn't move. His body glued in place.

"Kyle, come in. Are you okay? Is that Hadir?" Sam said in a frantic tone. Sam had been the one to alert him to Ella's approach.

As a former CIA agent himself, Sam was highly skilled, and Kyle trusted him to have his back. Sam's hostage-retrieval team had been in Afghanistan on assignment when Kyle enlisted Sam's technical expertise as a pilot so he could have a real-time view of the entire location in preparation for his meet with Hadir.

It had been through Hadir's intelligence that they'd been able to confirm that the man in the photo that former Scorpion team member Eddie Peterson had smuggled out of a war zone was indeed the person Hadir knew as Alhasan. And the man they believed to be the Fox. For the first time they had a name attached to the notorious terrorist.

Kyle couldn't get the last conversation he'd had with his asset out of his head. Hadir had told him Alhasan was preparing to move his entire operation. Their window to capture him was closing quickly. Was this the reason for tonight's meet? Did Hadir have the location for the move? His asset's message was so unusual that it had sent up all sorts of warning flags.

Kyle pulled his straying thoughts together. Too many people were counting on him staying alert.

With one final glance at the woman, he snatched up the radio. "It's not Hadir. It's a woman..." His voice trailed off. Although Lena and Sam had never met, Kyle had told him everything about his former CIA agent wife.

"A woman?" There was no mistaking Sam's surprise. "Who is she? And more important, what's she doing out here alone?"

Kyle wasn't able to voice his suspicions. "I have no idea," he managed while trying to shut out painful memories of his final moments with Lena. The argument they'd had. If only he'd known it was the last time he'd see her alive.

"I don't like this." Liz Ramirez, Kyle's second in command came on the radio. "Something's wrong, Kyle. Why would she be wandering around in the desert? This feels like a setup. We're on our way."

As much as he might agree, he couldn't allow it. Hadir had been very specific. "No, Liz, I've got this. I need you to stand down until I give the order."

Liz didn't respond, but Kyle could read all her doubts in the silence. He shared them.

He scrubbed his hand over his eyes. Being back in the field had opened up old wounds.

With Jase Bradford running the day-to-day operations for the team, Kyle had realized he missed the action of the field and wanted to be there when the team brought down the Fox once and for all. He had a personal stake in capturing the formidable enemy—he believed the Fox was responsible for Lena's death.

Still, nothing he'd seen to date prepared him for running into a woman who so strongly resembled Lena. He slammed the door on that possibility. He couldn't go there and survive having his heart torn to shreds again, because not a day went by that he didn't miss Lena terribly. Longed to have just another moment with her. Seeing this woman had brought all that back.

"Kyle, we're picking up at least four vehicles west of you. They're heading your way. Get out of there now," Sam yelled into the mic.

Kyle grabbed the binoculars and spotted dust boiling up on the western horizon beyond the compound. Liz was right. It felt like a setup.

He raced back to the unconscious woman and scooped her into his arms. He'd managed only a couple of steps before an explosion split the night and shook the ground beneath his feet. The blast dropped him to his knees. Shocked, he glanced at the compound near where he was to meet Hadir. It had exploded in a firestorm.

There was just enough time to cover Ella's body with his before a rush of ash and debris chased past them. Kyle could feel the heat from the explosion blast his back and embed bits of shrapnel into his exposed flesh.

In an instant, his misgivings for Hadir's safety doubled. If Hadir had been anywhere close to the compound, he wouldn't have survived…unless… An uninvited thought popped in his head, but he couldn't let it take life. He knew Hadir. They'd grown close through the months of working together. Hadir was desperate to get out of the life he'd lived in the past. He wouldn't sell Kyle out.

Kyle stumbled to his feet. Hauling Ella up with him, he charged for the Humvee. He deposited her in the seat, got in next to her and engaged the vehicle's starter. It didn't respond. He tried the radio, and his worst nightmare was confirmed. The explosion had taken out the Humvee's electrical system. They were now sitting ducks.

"Hurry, Liz," he murmured with urgency. Sam's team

would have picked up the explosion and Liz would dispatch a rescue team. Still, in the best-case scenario, it would take Liz twenty minutes to reach them from Bagram Air Force Base. That was the equivalent of a lifetime when facing off with an enemy. Anything could happen. He'd need some advantage to buy them time.

The woman beside him moaned softly and opened her eyes. She glanced around her surroundings and then to him. The second she saw him, she scooted as far away as possible. She was terrified.

I have to find him...

He didn't see her as a threat. Her injuries were too severe to be faked. She'd probably escaped from the compound, just in time to save her life. As the approaching vehicles drew closer, Kyle realized, like it or not, he'd need her help if they were to survive.

He unholstered his Glock. "Do you know how to shoot?" Her brows shot together. She appeared baffled by his question.

"There are enemy vehicles on the way here now. They'll reach us before help can arrive. So can you shoot?" His tone was short. Agitated.

She eyed him suspiciously before she answered. "Yes, I think so."

There was no time to wonder why she wouldn't know the answer off the top of her head. He grabbed the backup weapon he'd tucked under the seat and handed it to her. "We just have to stay alive until our exit team arrives. Okay?"

Fear chased across her face, and she shook her head. "I'm not leaving here. I won't desert him."

"Who are you talking about? If you want my help you'd better tell me."

She inched farther away, staring at him wide-eyed and tight-lipped.

"We have to move now," he ground out in frustration. With the enemy gaining quickly, they had to take cover behind the Humvee if they wanted a fighting chance.

Kyle grabbed her hand. Before he could move, she jerked free. He'd sort out the reasons why she was so terrified once they were safe.

"We're dead if we stay here. We have a chance if we take cover behind the Humvee." She hesitated a second longer then gave a short nod.

"Go ahead of me, I'll cover you. Stay low." Kyle barely got the words out before the lead vehicle reached them. Seconds later the world around them went up in gunfire.

With the enemy's headlights aimed straight at them, it was impossible to see anything. Kyle fired off a round in their direction to give her time to reach the rear of the vehicle.

There was no time to retrieve the M240 machine gun he'd stashed behind the backseat just in case. The enemy quickly retaliated and shots ricocheted off the open door he was standing behind, mere inches from his head. Kyle tucked and dived for the back as another barrage of bullets splintered the door off its hinges. If he'd been a second slower, he'd be dead.

God was watching out for him.

Ella leaned heavily against the Humvee's bumper as if the effort exerted by running to the back of the vehicle had taken its toll.

When he reached her side, she quickly straightened and moved away.

"Are you okay?" she asked when she got a good look at him. "Your back is burned and you're bleeding." She stared at him with those eyes. He realized she stood almost at eye level to him. She was tall like Lena, yet where Lena had been slim, this woman was suffering from extreme malnutrition.

"I'm fine," he managed. "I caught some of the debris from the explosion. The compound I'm guessing you came from must have been wired to detonate." Whatever her reason for wandering the desert, it might just have saved her life.

It took a second before what he said registered. Her hand flew to cover her trembling lips, immediately capturing his attention. An emotional reaction he couldn't relate to Lena. Lena had already been a top CIA operative by the time they'd met. Keeping her emotions in check was critical to her survival. The only time he'd seen his wife cry was when he'd had to deliver the news of her parents' deaths.

Another round of shots whizzed past the Humvee and they both ducked.

The additional vehicles came to a noisy halt next to the first, their high beams glaring. Kyle had no idea how many men they were up against. Adrenaline rushed through his body, buoying his courage. He'd almost forgotten how harrowing combat could be.

He flattened himself against the vehicle, fired quickly, then retreated. The noise of bullets striking metal was so loud it sounded like it was right next to them. Someone screamed in pain. He'd hit one of the enemy soldiers.

Out of the corner of his eye, he noticed Ella inching closer to the edge of the vehicle. She squared her shoulders and opened fire. Kyle couldn't take his eyes off her. She was clearly accustomed to using a gun.

Another round of gunfire shattered the front windshield and took out the back window. At this rate it wouldn't take long before the enemy realized they had the upper hand, if they didn't already. When that happened, they'd charge the vehicle. He and Ella would be dead.

With still no sign of the rescue chopper in sight, he had to come up with an alternate plan and fast.

"They're going to figure out it's just the two of us soon enough. We need to do something drastic," he yelled over the noise of the firefight.

As he watched, she swayed on her feet and he reached out to steady her. Immediately she backed away from him, the look in her eyes guarded.

Kyle covered his frustration with difficulty, because he was now genuinely concerned. "Are you okay?"

"Yes, I'm okay." Her voice, barely a whisper, did little to reassure him, yet the self-confidence she clearly didn't re-alize she possessed showed in the way she carried herself.

He'd seen the same determination and self-confidence in Lena. Except for that last mission. Something had been wrong from the beginning. His wife hadn't been herself.

Kyle shoved that dark memory aside. It had eaten at him for years. Now was not the time to rehash it.

"I'm okay," she insisted again when he appeared doubtful. "What do you have in mind?"

In spite of her assurances otherwise, he believed she couldn't handle much more. He needed to find out why she was here in the desert. To do so, they had to survive.

"If I can reach the backseat, I have an M240 machine gun there. It will give us a fighting chance until our backup arrives. I need you to cover me."

She checked her clip. "I'm almost empty."

He handed her his backup clip. "On the count of three." She nodded and he counted off. "One. Two. Three." He barely hit the final number when she opened fire. Even weak and barely hanging on, Ella handled herself like someone who had been in this situation before. And that didn't ease his mind one little bit. Had he managed to save one of Alhasan's agents?

Kyle dived through the busted rear window and crawled forward. It sounded like World War III outside, and he could hear charges whizzing past his head. He located the M240 and its rounds. With the weapon armed, he used the headrest for a stand. Shielding his eyes against the glare, he fired at the closest vehicle. The rounds shot from the weapon and instantly struck their target. The vehicle went up in flames. Screams followed. He'd injured at least one man, possibly more.

Without giving them time to regroup, Kyle continued firing, taking out two more vehicles.

He stopped briefly to listen. An engine fired. The remaining vehicle was in retreat.

He slid back through the rear window, still armed with the M240, and then stepped from the cover of the Humvee. As he continued firing at the retreating vehicle, some of the rounds hit the spare fuel container on the back and it exploded. The person behind the wheel swerved and lost control. The jeep flipped on its side and dug a ditch in the sand some ten feet long before it came to a grinding halt, dust seething.

Kyle rushed the vehicle. Two men were inside, unconscious and badly injured.

"Are they alive?" Ella asked from close behind him. He couldn't tell what response she was hoping for.

He nodded. "Yes, but just barely. We need to get them medical help right away. As well as the others." He glanced at the ruined vehicles surrounding them, then back to her. Ella hadn't budged. She was staring at the injured men. "Do you know them?" he asked curiously, and she whirled to face him.

"They were at the compound. They tried to kill me," she said without any sign of emotion.

Before he had time to process what she'd told him, the noise of additional approaching vehicles vibrated the ground at their feet. They were coming from the same direction as the others. Some sort of makeshift camp? If it was, it had been set up a good distance past the destroyed building in the western foothills of the mountains. They'd evacuated the compound because they'd planned to blow it up, which told him they'd known he was coming.

He started to head back to the Humvee when he noticed the way Ella was leaning over, her hands on her knees, her breathing hard. He touched her shoulder to warn her of the approaching vehicles and she rounded on him with the weapon drawn.

"Whoa," Kyle said and lifted both hands. "There's more vehicles on the way. We have to take cover."

She glanced over her shoulder briefly then back to him. She had the Glock aimed at his chest and she seemed torn. He held his breath while he wondered if he'd saved the life of an enemy combatant.

Would she shoot him? Could he reach her side and disarm her before she got a shot off? From what he'd seen so far, he knew she was deadly accurate.

"Ella, I'm not your enemy," he told her quietly and waited for some reaction. It felt like forever before she slowly lowered the Glock.

Kyle slung the M240 over his shoulder and they raced back to the Humvee barely reaching it before the vehicles came in firing heavily. Even with the M240 they wouldn't be able to hold them off for long.

Then in the distance, he heard it, like an answer to his prayer. Multiple choppers advancing their way. Liz would be piloting one of the machines, but she'd enlisted additional backup from Bagram, as well.

Thank You, God.

The Black Hawks ate up the distance quickly, their spotlights panning the desert surface until they spotted the enemy.

Two of the choppers homed in on newly arrived vehicles. A rapid exchange of fire ensued. Behind them, the remaining chopper tossed sand in their eyes as it landed.

"Hurry, sir," Agent Michael Harris yelled loud enough to be heard over the battle raging around them.

"We have to go, Ella," he told her. From her mutinous expression, Kyle realized he'd have a fight on his hands getting her on board. "We have about two minutes to board the chopper and get airborne before those guys behind us take out our only means of escape. The chopper can't stay on the ground much longer."

Still, she didn't budge. She stared at him in defiance. "I told you, I'm not going anywhere. I can't," she insisted with more emotion than he'd seen so far.

Whatever her reasons for wanting to stay, he wasn't about to leave her behind to face certain death. Kyle took the matter out of her hands and lifted her into his arms.

"No." She froze for half a beat and then she struggled with all her might to be free, her fists pummeling his chest. Kyle ignored her efforts completely as he headed for the chopper. A barely audible sob escaped as she gave up. Tears soaked his shirt.

His emotions were raw and on the surface. Her like-

ness to Lena had him off his game. Yet he wasn't prepared
to accept this woman as anything more than a prisoner
of war at the very least. She hadn't shot him when she'd
had the chance, but until he knew for certain where her
loyalties lay, he didn't trust her, and he certainly wasn't
letting her out of his sight.

Kyle raced to the Black Hawk as bullets whistled past
their heads. Michael took Ella from his arms and hauled
her into the chopper, where she quickly pushed his hands
away and huddled in one of the empty seats.

With her safely aboard, Kyle cleared the entrance and
the door was slammed shut. Seconds later, the Black
Hawk went airborne.

He took the seat next to Ella and glanced her way. She
scrubbed tears away with fisted hands. He didn't buy that
her being out there in the desert was an accident, but to
gain answers, he'd need her cooperation.

He handed her a set of headphones and put his on so
that he could try again to reach her. "Ella, let me help
you. Tell me who you're trying to save." Her only answer
was a brief shake of her head. His disappointment rose.

With Liz piloting the chopper, it made a ninety-degree
turn and headed back in the direction of Bagram. They'd
covered less than a quarter mile when a fireball lit up
the night sky. Liz used all her skills to avoid a direct hit.

Seconds later, the radio exploded. "I'm hit, I'm hit,"
a panicked voice—it sounded like Sam's pilot—shouted
into the mic, shocking the chopper's occupants.

"What's happening, Liz?" Kyle asked with urgency
as he leaned forward to get a clearer look. In shock he
watched Sam's chopper slowly drift to the ground.

"He must have taken our hit," Liz said in disbelief.

Kyle couldn't wrap his head around the fact that his friend's chopper had been shot from the sky.

"What were Sam and his team doing out here anyway?" Kyle asked in astonishment. As a civilian, Sam was forbidden to go out on military maneuvers.

"He insisted. They wanted to help," Liz replied over her shoulder.

Kyle closed his eyes and said a silent prayer for Sam and his team. He couldn't handle it if something happened to them because of him.

Liz veered back in the direction of the combat zone and Ella clutched the arms of her seat in a death grip.

Kyle struggled to keep his own fears from showing as he tried to reassure her. "It'll be okay. They need our help."

She stared at him with those soulful eyes. "You don't understand. It won't be okay."

Before he had the chance to ask what she meant, the chopper in front of theirs pinpointed the downed machine with its spotlight. Kyle watched in shock as a handful of men strong-armed the occupants of Sam's chopper into one of the waiting vehicles. With Sam's men so close to the enemy, his team couldn't risk shooting them from their chopper.

"Do we have a survivor count?" Kyle dreaded the answer. He didn't want to think about losing his friend like this.

"I counted five men other than enemy soldiers. Several are injured, but they all appear to be alive…for now," Michael added in an ominous tone.

Liz opened fire on one of the fleeing vehicles that didn't contain the hostages. The vehicle engaged right away and a surface-to-air missile barely missed them.

"Fall back, fall back," Kyle ordered as another missile came within a foot of taking out the second Black Hawk's main rotor blades. "We're outgunned. We don't stand a chance against those missiles."

"Sir, they're getting away." Michael turned to him in disbelief. "What do you want to do?"

Kyle prayed he wasn't making the worst mistake of his life—one that might cost Sam and his team theirs.

"Call Bagram. Get backup out here right away and have Booth and Dalton airborne...now. Once you've off-loaded us at the base, I want you and Liz on this, as well."

With his fear for Sam escalating, he ordered, "We have enemy soldiers on the ground. Have the remaining chopper land and make sure they haven't gotten away or been picked up. We need every man we can get on the ground. I want them questioned. One of them has to know something, and I want to know the second you have anything at all."

Kyle struggled to make sense of what had just happened. Why had the enemy risked coming after them so aggressively?

Ella. Somehow, it had to be because of her. She'd been at the compound. He couldn't get the fact that he'd clearly been set up out of his head. He trusted Hadir. He didn't believe his asset was responsible for what happened. That left the woman beside him.

I can't leave him. Was she talking about Alhasan? The idea settled uneasily in his mind. Was it possible she was somehow responsible for the ambush?

He saw her staring down at the nightmare below, her arms wrapped tight around her body in a self-defense gesture. Still, there was no doubt about it, she was important to Alhasan somehow. Only one question remained: Was she his prisoner or was she playing the part?

"You're safe now," he said. She didn't look at him.

Kyle's first instinct was to begin interrogating her right away. They had another witness to Alhasan's crimes. Yet from the way she'd reacted to him so far, he knew he wouldn't get anywhere by being aggressive. He'd have to go slow. She was barely keeping it together.

As hard as he tried, he couldn't get the similarities she shared with Lena out of his head, even if he wasn't prepared to accept them. It was ludicrous.

If she was Lena, where had she been for so long and who had he buried all those years earlier?

TWO

The Black Hawk churned dust and debris in its wake as it landed at the base's airstrip. Kyle had told Ella he would keep her safe, but he had no idea what he was up against or how close the enemy truly was. To save Joseph's life, could Ella follow through with what Alhasan demanded and become the enemy Kyle wouldn't suspect?

She'd had the opportunity in the desert and hadn't taken it. She could have killed Kyle with a single shot, yet some little niggling voice down deep in her heart wouldn't let her. She wasn't a killer. She was a missionary who trusted God to see her through. How could she take another life when it went against her Christian beliefs?

There was no doubt in her mind that Alhasan had deliberately blown up the compound to get rid of all traces of his crimes there and he didn't care if his men died in the process. He'd proven himself to be a ruthless killer.

If she didn't do as he asked, Joseph would die. It was an impossible choice to make.

She'd lost her heart to the boy the moment she held him in her arms. She'd named him Joseph because…well, she couldn't remember why, only that she'd just always loved the name.

Alhasan had told her the boy belonged to the woman who shared her cell. He'd enjoyed going over the graphic details of how he'd killed the woman because she refused to do what he wanted. He'd driven the point home.

Now it was her turn. That she'd escaped the compound seconds before it went up, and ran into Kyle only to have him offer her shelter was no coincidence. It reeked of Alhasan's scheming.

He'd be watching, expecting her to follow his orders and infiltrate the Scorpion team by any means necessary so that she could gain access to their headquarters. Then she was to take out the entire eight-member unit. Even though he hadn't said as much, she believed there was something important he needed. Through all the years of trying to brainwash her, Alhasan's rage toward the Scorpion team had always seemed a bit too personal. There was something else going on. She'd pressed him for more answers once. Incensed, he'd insisted she knew all she needed to do her part. And that if she didn't, Joseph would die.

"Ready?" Kyle's gravelly voice interrupted her troubled thoughts. Shivers sped down her spine, and Ella steeled herself to face her rescuer.

Their gazes tangled, and she sucked in a breath. As she stared into what seemed to her familiar gray eyes, she couldn't answer. She struggled to hold on to the faintest of memories the worry on his face sparked. But it was as fleeting as dust in the wind.

"You'll be safe here," he assured her, his warm breath fanning her cheek. If only that were true. She couldn't imagine a time when she didn't feel hunted.

He jumped from the chopper with its engine still running and held out his hand to help her out. After years of surviving unspeakable torture, she'd learned that human touch always resulted in pain. Joseph's gentle hugs were the only type of contact she could bear anymore. Would it always be this way?

She ignored his hand and jumped to the ground, the effort sending jolts of agony through her damaged body.

"Let's get you to the hospital," he said after a moment. "Once the doctor takes a look at you we'll talk more."

"That's not necessary. I just want to…" She looked away. Ella fought back despair. She had to stay strong for Joseph. She'd find a way to save the boy.

She tucked a stray hair behind her ear, her fingers rough against her skin. Beside her, Kyle pulled in an audible breath. What had she done? Did he find her appearance repulsive?

Her hair was clumped with dirt and dried blood. Her skin as dry as the desert. Her face slashed. She couldn't even imagine how bad she must look. She hadn't seen a mirror in years and she'd lost track of her injuries. The scars over scars. She held her palms up. The crippling pain she'd endured always resurfaced when she thought about the pleasure Alhasan had taken in removing her fingerprints. That was the last time she'd cried until today.

As if reading her thoughts, Kyle stopped and turned to her. "You're beautiful, Ella. And no amount of torture inflicted by a person lacking in humanity can take that from you."

She closed her eyes. She didn't trust his kindness. She'd give just about anything to let down her guard for a second. Trust another human being to be kind. Believe Kyle when he told her he could keep her safe. She couldn't.

She shook her head. "Kyle, I…" She glanced up and stopped when she got a good look at his shell-shocked expression.

"What is it?" What had she said?

"How did you know my name?" he uttered in astonishment, and she realized she'd slipped up. He had no idea that thanks to Alhasan, she knew lots of things about him and the rest of the Scorpions.

"I don't know. Someone must have mentioned it."

She could see him struggling to recall the possibility.

"The base has some of the best doctors on staff," he said absently. "You'll be in good hands here."

They reached the hospital and he went inside and waited for her. With nothing left to do, she followed him in and glanced around nervously. She'd just get her injuries treated and then she'd leave the base. They couldn't hold her against her will. She'd find Joseph and save him, because there was no way she could take so many innocent lives, especially Kyle's.

A midfifties man wearing a doctor's coat tossed over his fatigues came forward to greet them as if he'd been expecting them. He hid his shock at Ella's appearance with difficulty.

"I'm Dr. Anderson," he said with a kindly smile. "I heard you two had a close call out there in the desert. We have a team out there now," he told Kyle.

"Is there any news yet?" Kyle asked.

The doctor shook his head. "No, I'm sorry, there isn't. They just arrived at the scene of the attack. It could take a while."

Kyle turned to Ella. "Doctor, this is Ella Weiss. She managed to escape from the compound before it went up."

The doctor nodded in appreciation. "I'd say someone

was looking out for you. If you'll come with me, let's take a look at your injuries." When she hesitated he added, "I promise I'm going to take good care of you." The doctor glanced at Kyle's bloody and burned back. "Once I'm finished with Ella, I'd like to take a look at those injuries, Agent Jennings."

Kyle shook his head, dismissing the request. "I'm fine. Look after her. She needs you the most."

The doctor reluctantly nodded.

Ella hugged her arms around her body. She wore her mistrust like a well-worn coat. With one final glance Kyle's way, she followed the doctor, but not before she noticed the frown on Kyle's face. A look that jumped out of her memory as if she'd seen it yesterday. If only she could understand how that was possible.

With so many questions rattling around in his head, letting Ella go was difficult. He didn't understand why she had been so determined not to leave the desert. Who was she protecting? Yet if he'd learned anything while being in her company this short time, it was that he had to move slowly. She carried around more than the physical scars on her body.

He glanced at his watch and his impatience multiplied. Treading slow was not in his DNA. Especially now, when every second that slipped by without answers meant the chances for rescuing Sam and his team alive were slim. Alhasan had dozens of hidden tunnels beneath the desert surface that allowed him a fast escape.

Kyle's body ached from the minor injuries he'd sustained in the blast. He was mentally exhausted. Thinking clearly had become a near-impossible task. He needed sleep, but with so many lives on the line such a luxury would have to wait.

It felt like hours had passed before he spotted Dr. Anderson heading his way. He shoved aside his uneasiness over Sam's safety and got to his feet.

"Is she okay?" he asked gravely. From the frown on the man's face, he expected the news to be dire.

"Surprisingly yes, considering what she's been through. She's suffering from severe malnutrition and dehydration." The doctor shook his head. "I've given her IV fluids for that."

So far, nothing the doctor said was surprising. It had probably been years since she'd had a decent meal. "Did she tell you anything about what happened to her?" If she wouldn't talk to him, perhaps she would confide in her doctor.

"No. In fact, it took a whole lot of convincing for her to allow us to treat her injuries. What I can tell you is they are consistent with someone who's suffered years of abuse."

Kyle couldn't imagine the terrible things she'd gone through. He'd known her only a short time, yet he'd glimpsed a will to live that not even Alhasan's torture could destroy. Just like Lena. But she wasn't Lena, and he couldn't accept her resemblance to his wife as anything more than a coincidence.

Still, he had no proof she was Ella Weiss, either, and he wasn't going to simply accept her word for who she was. The real Ella might be dead. Alhasan could have groomed her to pretend to be the woman.

An idea occurred and he asked, "Do you have the means to do a DNA test, doctor?" He needed positive confirmation she was who she said. His only hope for an ID was if Ella's DNA was on file somewhere back in the United States, or perhaps they could track down her dental records.

The doctor watched him closely. "No, I'm sorry, we don't. I can do the swab and send it wherever you'd like me to." He paused for a lengthy beat. "I'm guessing Ella's been missing for many years. Are there any family members left to test her DNA against?"

Kyle had no idea. If they couldn't test her DNA, how could they positively confirm her story?

The doctor obviously noticed his disappointment. "I'll do the swab. Hopefully an opportunity will arise."

Kyle smiled his gratitude. "Is it okay if I speak with her?"

"Of course. She's in the last room on your right. I've rounds to finish. I'll do the swab once I'm done. Try not to keep her awake too long, though. She's exhausted. Rest will be the best medicine possible."

Kyle turned to leave and then remembered something he'd wanted to ask. "Doctor, can you tell me if Ella has a birthmark on her left shoulder?"

The question took the doctor by surprise. "I beg your pardon?"

He needed someone else to confirm she wasn't Lena. If Ella didn't possess the same birthmark as his wife, he'd have his proof once and for all. "Does Ella have a small, thumb-size birthmark on her left shoulder?"

"No, but then again, she has a lot of scars." The expected relief didn't come. Something akin to disappointment made it impossible to answer.

The doctor's phone rang and he glanced down at it. "I must go. I'll check in on Ella later."

Finding out what she knew about Alhasan was critical. Hadir's indications were certainly ominous enough and Sam and his team's lives were on the line.

Kyle stopped outside her room and gathered his tumultuous thoughts. He noticed the door stood ajar. A male voice came from inside the room. Was one of the medical personnel with Ella? The man sounded agitated. A strangled whimper caught his attention and he shoved the door open in time to see a man standing over Ella, choking her.

Charging to her bedside, Kyle jerked the assailant off her. The man reacted with all the fury of a caged animal. He lunged for Kyle with a knife. They scuffled back and forth.

Kyle slammed his fist hard into the man's face and he went crashing back against the door. The knife slid from his hand. Kyle went for the man once more, but he reached for a nearby chair and slung it at Kyle's head. He ducked and the edge of the chair grazed his right side. The force sent him stumbling backward.

His assailant took advantage, grabbed the knife and raced from the room. Kyle heard someone outside scream, "He has a knife!"

He stumbled to Ella's side. "Did he hurt you?" His first concern was for her safety. She clutched her throat and coughed and gasped for air.

Somehow, she nodded. "I'm okay."

While he wasn't completely convinced, the assailant was getting away. Kyle bolted from the room.

One of the medical personnel pointed to the emergency door. "He went that way."

Kyle hit the door full force. Outside, he did a 360-degree turn. The man had disappeared into thin air. The most concerning part of the attack was that it had happened in the middle of the day at a heavily guarded military base. It was both brazen and desperate, further emphasizing what he believed. Ella was of grave importance to Alhasan.

Kyle rushed back inside. "Call the MPs. We need the base locked down. Now," he told one of attending doctors.

The man grabbed his phone to issue the order while Kyle hurried to Ella's room. Dr. Anderson was there with her.

"She's all right," Anderson assured him. "But I don't understand how that man got on the base so easily. Especially with a weapon."

That was a good question. Did the assailant have someone on the inside who let him onto the base? Kyle believed Ella might know the answer by the way she wouldn't look at him.

"Doctor, do you mind if I have a moment alone with Ella?"

Dr. Anderson hesitated briefly before agreeing. "I'll be right back." He smiled at Ella and left them alone.

Kyle waited until the door closed. "What happened?"

For the longest time he doubted if she would respond. "I'm not sure," she said at last. "He just barged in and started choking me."

After what happened in the desert, he was positive this was no random attack. Ella had been deliberately targeted.

"Did you recognize him? What did he say to you?" he asked. She shook her head, still without looking at him. From body language alone he could see she knew more than she was saying. He didn't understand her unwillingness to cooperate. Unless... The thought was unspeakable.

"Ella, help me out here. What's going on? Why are

they trying to kill you? You must know something," he insisted as gently as he could manage.

Her brown eyes flashed anger, reminding him once more of Lena when she was arguing a cause she believed in. Like the last mission she'd signed up for. The one he hadn't wanted her to go on.

Don't go down that rabbit hole. She's not Lena.

"Ella, please. Let me help you," he implored quietly.

"No." The word tore from her. "I don't need your help and I can't help you. I just want to forget this whole thing ever happened. I want to leave." Her mutinous gaze slammed into his.

Kyle's patience reached the breaking point. "You can't pretend this didn't happen. There's a reason why they risked coming after you on a heavily guarded military base. You know something they don't want made public. They can't afford to let you live."

Ella recoiled at his directness. "You don't know what you're talking about. He wasn't trying to kill me, he was..." She'd said more than she intended.

"He was warning you," Kyle guessed, and she turned away. "What do they want you to do?"

Ella stared at the wall. She had clammed up tight and wasn't going to answer any more of his questions.

It took everything inside him to let the matter go for the moment. He was getting nowhere right now, and the last thing she needed was his irritation.

Kyle noticed her body silently quaking. Was she crying? He'd hurt her. Regret ripped through him.

She was hurting. She was like a wounded child. Whatever her true identity was, whoever she was protecting, she needed someone she could trust, and he'd give anything to be that person. The desire to take her in his arms and hold her while she cried was strong, but he still didn't know for certain if she was a victim or the enemy.

"You should rest now," he said in a voice rough with unexplored emotion. "I'll stay with you until you fall asleep. I promise, we're going to figure this out."

Something in what he said must have gotten to her. She stared at him with what appeared to be minute hope. He'd give anything to understand the battle he saw raging in her, but if he ever wanted the chance to do so, he'd have to learn something he wasn't good at, and quickly. Patience.

When he was satisfied she slept, he stepped out into the hall. If he couldn't get answers from Ella, he'd check in with Liz in hopes that she had some positive news.

But Liz's update could not have been more discouraging. She and Michael were on the ground along with the rest of the in-country team and taking an active part in the interrogations of the wounded prisoners.

"We had the location where we believed Alhasan's men might have taken Sam's team, but we were too late. They'd moved them."

Not the news he wanted to hear. "Any sign of Hadir?" he asked. His gut told him too much time had passed for Hadir to still be alive.

Liz's lengthy pause did little to ease his mind. "I'm sorry to have to tell you this, Kyle, but we found the body of a man some distance from the compound." She hesitated for a second, and he knew Hadir was gone. "I was able to confirm it was Hadir. It appears he was shot in the head at close range. He'd been dead for a while."

Hadir was dead. He couldn't believe it. Grief made it hard to think clearly, much less get words to come forth.

Kyle thought back to the first time he'd met the man.

He had been the one to talk Hadir into helping the team out with the promise that once he'd fulfilled his end of the bargain, he would be able to start a new life in the United States. Hadir had died because of his allegiance to Kyle and the Scorpions.

"He was planning a new life," he muttered in disgust.

"I know. I'm sorry, Kyle. I know you two were close."

A chilling thought occurred. If Hadir was dead, then who had sent the message? Had he been deliberately sent out to the desert to be ambushed?

Kyle struggled to keep back the emotions. "Thanks." He could tell from Liz's tone that more bad news followed. He closed his eyes. "What else?"

"Michael has been monitoring Alhasan's recruiting website. He thought there might be some news on what happened today. Kyle, there's a message there I think you should see."

"Hang on." Kyle brought up the website on the phone. What he saw chilled him to the bone and filled him with more doubts.

A photo showed Hadir slumped over and clearly dead from a gunshot wound to the head. A message taped to his chest read This Is What We Do to Traitors, Ella.

Alhasan mentioned Ella by name. What if Ella was actually one of them? Was their chance meeting deliberate? The thought was unsettling.

He returned to the call. "We need to find Sam now. If this is what Alhasan does to his own people, I can't imagine what he'll put Sam and his men through. Let me know the minute you have anything," he told Liz and then disconnected the call.

With his friend's life weighing on his conscience, Kyle slipped back into Ella's room. She hadn't budged. He sat quietly by her bed and opened the pocket Bible he kept with him always. He felt unsettled. He let the word of God comfort him.

Growing up and through most of his adult life, he hadn't believed in anything beyond the job. Losing Lena had changed that. Her death had brought him to his knees. He'd hit rock bottom. There was nowhere else for him to turn except to God, and he was grateful every day of his life that he had.

He closed the Bible and stared at the sleeping woman. Why couldn't he reach her? He was running out of time and options. There was a timetable on Sam's and his men's lives. Bringing them home safely depended on him figuring out what Ella was keeping from him.

I have to find him...

Alhasan's message made it clear if she didn't do as he asked, he'd kill her like he had Hadir. What was Alhasan expecting her to do? No matter what the truth was, he was positive it would destroy both her life and the lives of many others.

Was her refusal to cooperate with Kyle proof enough that she was planning to do what Alhasan wanted, either against her will or otherwise? She hadn't said as much, but he was certain Alhasan was using someone she cared about to ensure Ella completed her task, and he obviously had men watching her. He'd certainly proven he could get to her any time he wanted, at least while she was here in Afghanistan.

He pulled out his phone and did a search on her name. He'd need to find out as much as he could about Ella Weiss. Was she real, or just an alias cooked up to fulfill a part in Alhasan's deadly game?

THREE

"*Ella! Help me!*" *Someone screamed her name and she turned. Joseph! Something was terribly wrong. Joseph was terrified.*

She reached for the boy and drew him into her arms. She could feel him trembling. Before she could reassure him, ask what was wrong, someone jerked him from her arms.

Alhasan. "I told you what would happen if you didn't do your part, Ella. It's time for him to die and it's all because of you."

"No!" she screamed. Panic welled inside her. She had to save Joseph.

She could hear the boy's desperate shrieks as Alhasan dragged him from the room.

Ella charged after them like a mother bear protecting her cub, but she was too late. The door slammed in her face. The lock slid in place. Joseph was gone and it was her fault.

Beyond the prison door, she heard Alhasan's disgusting laugh. She'd lost Joseph, the one thing that had kept her going, and it amused him.

"No. Please, no. I'll do what you want. Please don't

hurt him," she screamed and slammed her clenched fists against the steel door. But as always, Alhasan was just out of her reach. If she could reach him, she would make him pay for hurting Joseph.

Someone grabbed her and held her tight. She couldn't move. She struggled with all her strength to be free but it was useless. Yet unlike all those times in the past, the arms that held her now were gentle. Strong. Familiar...

Her eyes flew open and she stared into piercing gray eyes as stormy as the sea. For a second it threw her until she realized it wasn't one of Alhasan's men who held her. It was Kyle. Past cruelty had her pushing frantically against his chest until he let her go. The remnants of the dream were still close and so real that she struggled to find calm.

"It's okay. You were having a bad dream," he assured her. She searched his face, wondering how much she'd given away. He didn't know the truth. Everything about the dream was real except for Joseph's fate. She still had time to change that.

Just for a heartbeat, in a moment of weakness, she considered telling Kyle about Joseph. If she did, if she enlisted his help, would she be sealing Joseph's fate? She didn't dare take that risk.

Compassion softened some of the tautness from his mouth. "I know you're hurting and I'm sorry. I wish I could take it all away." She saw the answer in his eyes and she wanted to cry. He was being so kind. Would that change once he knew what her purpose was?

"It's so unfair," she murmured and turned away. She was talking about the boy, but he clearly thought she meant herself. She shoved the terrifying dream of Joseph as far back into her anxious mind as she could. She couldn't think about what might be happening to the boy and not go crazy.

"Ella, I promise we'll figure out what happened to you. If you have family somewhere, we'll find them together." His voice caught over those words and she glanced up at him curiously. He'd been so strong for her, and yet she sensed that he struggled with his own unsettled past. He'd lost someone. His grief had left an indelible mark on his life.

She glanced around the empty C-17. It was just the two of them on board. The unknown that lay ahead for her was nothing compared to the fear that gripped her heart every time she thought about what she'd left behind.

When Kyle first told her he was taking her to the United States, she'd fought him every step of the way. She couldn't bear the thought of putting an ocean between herself and Joseph. She remembered overhearing Alhasan talking to the American about moving their operation to the United States. She believed Alhasan would want to be close to her to make sure she did as he requested. He'd bring Joseph with him as leverage. There was still a chance.

Outside her window, the ground beneath them approached at a rapid pace. The plane touched down hard and then taxied to a stop on a small airstrip in a rural area.

You have one week to fulfill your purpose or the boy dies. The man who'd attacked her had relayed Alhasan's deadly message. Two days had passed already. The clock was ticking. Yet as hard as she tried to convince herself she could do what Alhasan asked, doubts and insecurities crowded in. She wasn't a killer. Could she go against everything she believed in to save Joseph?

She realized Kyle had asked her something, but she'd been too caught up in her concerns to hear. He'd kept a watchful eye on her, never once leaving her side during her stay at Bagram.

When he'd first told her that after an extensive computer search, he'd found out she was from a small town in West Virginia called Mountain Song, where he would be taking her, she hadn't been able to hide her terror. He had no way of knowing it was all because of the mistake *she'd* made. She should have tried to convince him to take her straight to Scorpion headquarters. Should have fulfilled the mission Alhasan asked her to do. But she'd failed and now she was terrified Joseph would pay the ultimate price.

"Ella?" There was real concern on his face as he continued to watch her.

She shook her head because she couldn't seem to find the words to lie. Everything was far from all right.

"It's this way," Kyle said once they'd disembarked. He pointed to a light-colored SUV in the near-empty parking lot of the Darden County Airport. He headed that way and she followed.

She watched him retrieve the keys from the fender well and then unlocked the vehicle.

Kyle held the passenger door open for her. It was then that she noticed something for the first time, and it stopped her dead in her tracks. He wore a wedding band on his left hand. She couldn't take her eyes off it. She…recognized it. A fragmented memory disappeared before she could claim it. She didn't understand it. She absently touched her left ring finger and tried to hold on to the memory.

"Is something wrong?" he asked when he spotted her staring at the ring.

Stunned, Ella shook her head. How did she recognize his wedding ring?

Kyle searched for the truth in her eyes. Time lost its importance as something shifted between them. Right there in the middle of the parking lot, the moment turned intimate. She'd seen that same look...before.

Wait, how did she know that? As she struggled to untangle the truth, the color of his eyes turned to charcoal.

Suddenly it was hard to catch her breath, and Ella looked away. She couldn't explain the confusing memories, but they didn't matter. She had to keep her focus on saving Joseph's life.

Once she was inside the SUV, he got behind the wheel and they left the airport.

Although he didn't say as much, she could tell Kyle was concerned by the way he constantly checked the rearview mirror as if expecting trouble. Her uneasiness doubled. Had something happened?

She tried to let go of her fears as the rolling countryside passed her by. She put down her window. The air was crisp and fresh and carried just a hint of the winter to come. It was nothing like the dry desert breeze she'd left behind.

Soon, the scenic woods faded and the small, picturesque Southern town of Mountain Song spread out before them.

During the flight, Kyle had filled in some of the more personal details of her life. He'd told her she was a missionary, but she'd known that. Alhasan had said as much. What she hadn't realized was that she'd been in the field for years.

According to Kyle, she'd met her fiancé, David, during one of her trips to Afghanistan. At the time she had been working with the homeless there, providing food and medicine. Kyle said her father had pastored one of the local churches in Mountain Song for most of Ella's life. Both her father and mother as well as David and several other members of the church had gone on that fateful mission trip with Ella. None had returned alive.

Why did nothing about her life story make sense? Was it just because of the severity of the injury she'd suffered, or the years of torture and brainwashing?

Doubt churned inside her as they passed through town and Kyle pulled into the parking lot of a church from by-gone days.

"This is where your father pastored," he said quietly, and Ella turned to look at the simple white steeple shooting up into a cloudy afternoon sky, hoping something would ring a bell but not finding it.

The building itself held the quiet majesty of another time period. She noticed a historical marker on the front of the sanctuary and wondered how many troubled souls had passed through those doors to seek redemption. Kyle mentioned the original sanctuary had been standing for several hundred years.

He turned off the ignition and angled toward her. "Are you ready for this?" She knew he was only trying to help her regain her past, but all she could think about was the boy she'd left behind in Afghanistan. His life was now measured in days.

The nervousness in her stomach assured her she wasn't anywhere close to being ready. She was terrified. Nothing about what she'd seen so far of the town where she'd grown up sparked any recollection. Why couldn't she remember her hometown? Her family? Her life?

Kyle had told her he'd found someone from her past by the name of Tracy Cartwright. The church's secretary had been good friends with her parents and worked with her father. Tracy was waiting inside for her now. Uncertainty crept in. What if she wasn't Ella Weiss at all but really a cold-blooded killer?

She prayed for strength and found it. She'd get through this meeting, find a way to convince Kyle to take her to the Scorpions' headquarters, and then it would be up to her to save Joseph.

Ella slowly looked at Kyle. She'd only known him for a short period of time, and yet he made her feel safe. Protected. Cared for.

She watched him swallow noticeably and then touch her cheek. For the first time she didn't want to pull away. Was it just because of she was afraid of what waited for her inside and needed his strength? Her breath quickened in the warmth of his gaze and her thoughts drifted to things she couldn't remember. What did it feel like to be kissed? To be touched by someone who wasn't intent on hurting her.

Somewhere a horn blasted and the spell was broken. Heat crept up her neck and she moved away. For a moment…well, she'd let emotions get in the way. She couldn't afford to do that ever again. Being in control was all that kept her alive.

A handful of awkward seconds passed before Kyle got out of the vehicle and came round to open her door.

They walked side by side into the sanctuary and Ella couldn't think of a single thing to say to fill the void.

The moment she stepped inside and looked around, she realized nothing about the quiet old southern church felt like the home she longed for. Ella struggled to keep her disappointment from showing. She'd foolishly hoped everything would just instantly fall into place and her memory would return.

"Why don't we wait for them up front? It looks peaceful there," Kyle said to her silence. "After everything that's happened recently, I think we both could use a little peace."

They headed down the center aisle lined with dark wooden pews that smelled of polish. There were hymnals in the seats. Up in front stood an altar with the carved words *do this in remembrance of me.*

The podium where the minister delivered his message captured her attention. Her father would have stood in that very spot each week. She closed her eyes and tried to imagine him, but she couldn't even bring up his face.

She was aware of Kyle standing beside her, watching her carefully. Was he expecting some flicker of recognition? They both realized that at some point the pieces of her life should start to fall into place if she really was who he thought she was.

A side door opened and two people, one a mid-thirties-looking man and the other a woman who appeared to be in her forties, entered the sanctuary.

The man stepped forward, smiled and introduced himself. "James Montgomery, I'm the pastor. And this is Tracy Cartwright, our church clerk." The pastor turned to the woman by his side.

Tracy barely acknowledged the introductions. She appeared to have suffered a terrible shock. She covered her trembling mouth with her hand.

The pastor squeezed the woman's shoulder then spoke to Ella. "Tracy and your mother were good friends. Losing her was hard. *This* is hard."

Tracy came over to Ella and stared at her for the longest time, then she took her into her arms and squeezed her tight. "I can't believe it's you. Oh, Ella, you're alive. You're alive. I'm so glad."

Ella stiffened and fought back the usual revulsion whenever anyone got too close.

While Tracy continued to hug her close and weep in earnest, Ella wondered why she couldn't remember her. She was clearly a family friend.

Slowly, she untangled herself from Tracy's grasp.

The woman had tears streaming down her face. "Do you remember me at all?" she asked with a hopeful look on her face.

Ella shook her head. "I'm sorry, I don't." She turned to Kyle for the assurances he was quick to give.

"It's okay," Kyle assured her. "With everything you've been through, it may take some time for your memory to return in full. You just have to be patient."

"Oh, I can't believe it," Tracy exclaimed and touched the ring that Ella still wore around her neck. "Your engagement ring survived. You were so proud of that ring when David gave it to you. And your mother and father were thrilled when you and David announced you two were getting married. Your mother said you were the perfect couple, with you both being missionaries and all." Tracy leaned over and kissed her cheek.

It took every ounce of strength she could muster not to move away. Accepting human kindness as genuine was a near-impossible feat. She'd long forgotten there were nice people in the world.

"Is it okay if I speak with Tracy alone?" Ella asked Kyle, because there were so many questions she needed answered.

"Of course. I'll wait for you by the door." She watched as both Kyle and the pastor headed for the back of the church.

Once they were alone Tracy indicated the front pew and they sat together. Now that it was just the two of them, Ella wasn't sure what she wanted to know, so she asked the first thing that came to mind.

"What were they like?"

Tracy smiled a watery smile. "Your mom was sweet and kind and one of the best people I've ever met. Your father the same. They complemented each other well. They were strong in their faith and would do anything to help a person in need. They certainly helped me enough."

Tracy's description didn't really fill in any of the blanks. Being a Christian couple who served in a leadership position at the church, it stood to reason they'd both be caring people. "Do you have a photo of them?"

"Oh, yes, I do," she said as if she'd forgotten. "I brought it with me. I thought it might help you remember them. You can keep it." She reached in her pocket and brought out a photo and handed it to Ella. "This was taken right before you all left for Afghanistan, more than eight years ago. It shows everyone who went on the trip. You had barely been in Afghanistan a couple of weeks when the attack happened. The bodies of several members of the group were recovered. You, David and your parents were never located," Tracy whispered in a shaky voice.

Ella stared down at the people captured in a moment in time.

Tracy pointed to the older couple in the middle. "This is your mother, Betty, and your father, Steve, and that's you next to them with David."

Her parents. She didn't recognize them or her fiancé.

Alhasan had taken pleasure in telling her that his men had attacked her mission team and killed everyone except for her. Ella had life threatening injuries, but instead of killing her right away, he'd thought she might be useful to his cause someday so he'd spared her life.

Ella shook her head. She had no way of knowing if anything he told her was true.

Her attention was drawn to the photo of the woman she'd been back then. Smiling. Happy. Healthy. Her hair long like it was now. Dressed in a cheerful sweater and jeans, she wore the same silver studs as she did today.

"They were so proud of you and the work you were doing," Tracy said and patted her hand.

Yet the woman in the photo was a stranger. Right now, Ella couldn't imagine being that happy again.

She stumbled to her feet. She needed air. Kyle must have sensed she was in trouble, because he hurried down the aisle to her side. She was barely hanging on.

Tracy got to her feet, as well. "Oh, honey, I'm so sorry. I didn't mean to upset you. I know your memory is a bit fuzzy, but don't you worry. It'll come back. Once you're at your parents' house and settled in, everything will fall into place. You'll see."

Ella stared at her in confusion. "My parents' house?"

"Well, yes. The one at the lake. You remember," Tracy added and then realized what she'd said and looked away. "I'm sorry, that was silly of me. What I meant was your parents owned a house at Mountain Song Lake. I bought it a few years back when it came up for sale. I just couldn't stand to see it go to a stranger. Now I rent it out from time to time to tourists. Other than that, it's been sitting there all those years just waiting for..." She didn't finish.

Ella couldn't manage an answer. Her brain felt as if it

might explode with all things she'd learned. If only they made sense.

"I thought you could use it until you figured out what you wanted to do," Tracy added sympathetically.

Once more she turned to Kyle for help, and he didn't disappoint.

"Being in your former home might help you pull some of the pieces together," he said in that no-nonsense way he had of cutting through the clutter of a conversation.

Tracy's expression lightened. "Then it's settled. Why don't I just get the spare key?" She hurried away without an answer.

Ella barely waited until she was out of earshot. "I can't do this," she whispered in a frantic tone. "I can't go there. I don't belong here." When she looked at Kyle, the strength she'd seen in him since that first day in the desert seeped deep inside her like a warm cup of cocoa on a cold day.

"This is exactly where you need to be," he assured her. "Give it time. Your memories will return, and I'll be right here with you when they come back. You're not alone any longer, and I won't let him hurt you anymore."

Tracy returned a few minutes later and handed Ella the key. "I stop by from time to time to tidy up, so the place should be clean." She gave them directions. "When I heard you were coming back home, I stocked the fridge and pantry for you."

When Ella couldn't manage a response, Kyle was there for her. "Thanks for the use of the house and for your hospitality." He turned to Ella. "Can you give us a minute?" She nodded slowly and Kyle led Tracy a little ways away and spoke with her briefly.

She couldn't hear the discussion, but Tracy didn't appear pleased by it.

After a second longer they rejoined her and the pastor. "I'd like to talk to you more at a later time, if I may?" he asked Tracy.

"Of course," she managed after a second, then dug in her purse and handed him a card. "My cell number is there along with the phone number here. You can reach me at one of those numbers anytime."

"Thanks." Kyle glanced at Ella. "Why don't we get you settled in?"

Once they were outside, Ella could no longer keep her worries to herself. "I don't understand why I can't remember anything she just told me." She pulled out the photo. "Tracy showed me this photo of my parents and my fiancé. I don't recognize them. How can I not recognize my own parents?"

She felt herself sinking in despair when he stepped closer. He didn't touch her again, and yet she could feel his calming personality quieting her frayed nerves. "You've been through more than most people could survive in a lifetime. Cut yourself some slack and don't expect the memories to just automatically return. It could take a while."

She wished she could believe what he said, but she didn't. For the longest time she didn't answer as she struggled to keep the hopelessness at bay.

Something soft and wet touched her face, capturing her attention. Ella stared up at the sky in wonderment. Tiny snowflakes had begun to fall.

"What is it?" With a bewildered frown, Kyle glanced up, as well.

"It's snowing," she said in amazement.

Some of the worry eased from his face and he smiled. She hadn't seen him smile since she'd met him, and yet she couldn't get over the feeling that she recognized it from…somewhere.

Alhasan's photos of each of the eight member Scorpion team had been taken during what appeared to be combat situations.

"It is," Kyle said in agreement.

"I can't remember the last time I've seen it snow. It must have been…" She remembered a cabin in the mountains. Snow falling. Someone else was there with her. It was… The memory disappeared and she closed her eyes trying to recapture it. In her heart she knew it was real and important, but it was gone.

"What month is it?" she asked puzzled. She'd been gone for years. She had no idea what day it was, even.

"It's December 13. It's almost Christmas."

Christmas! Tears stung her eyes and she squeezed her hands into fists to fight them. "I remember…" She stopped. Who was the person at the cabin with her?

"What?" he asked with urgency, as if her answer was the most important thing in the world to him.

Her face creased into a frown. "I don't know."

All around them were the sounds of small-town life. People talking. A car honking. Children laughing. All things that should make her feel at home, only they left her empty inside.

With one final glance at the sky, Kyle said, "It's getting colder out. Let's get you warm."

They were halfway to the SUV when the sound of tires squealing close by captured her attention. Kyle whirled at the same time as Ella. A nondescript beige car with blacked-out windows charged through the parking lot straight for them.

"Run," he yelled and grabbed Ella's hand, all but hauling her along with him to the vehicle. They'd just reached the cover of the SUV when the occupants of the car opened fire.

Kyle pushed her behind one of the SUV's massive tires. "Stay as low as you can." He dropped down next to her, pulled out his Glock and eased forward until he had a clear shot.

Ella leaned forward in time to see the armed man in the passenger seat duck down quickly to avoid being shot. The driver did the same but not before she got a good look at him. It was Alhasan.

Her gut knotted in fear. He'd managed to track her here. How had he found them? Another far more disturbing thought raced through her head, seemingly confirming her earlier suspicions. Had it all been a lie? Had he deliberately put her in Kyle's path, staged her escape even, so that she could be used as bait to kill Kyle and draw out the rest of the team? If that were true, then there would be no second chance for her or Joseph. They had both been nothing more than a means to accomplish his deadly end.

Ella screamed and covered her ears as bullets from multiple automatic weapons took out the SUV's engine and riddled holes along its side.

Kyle spotted the pastor and Tracy on the steps of the church and he feared they'd catch a straying bullet. "Go back inside. Call 911," he yelled and they rushed into the sanctuary.

The car brazenly came to a stop a few feet from the

side of their SUV. Kyle glanced at Ella. She was visibly terrified. He eased closer. If they wanted her dead, they'd have to take him out first.

He could hear a heated argument followed by a door opening. Then footsteps. He pushed Ella farther behind the cover of his body as a man cleared the front of the vehicle. Kyle didn't give him time to spot them before he opened fire. The weapon flew from the man's hand and he screamed in pain as the bullet struck his chest. He stumbled backward and onto the asphalt.

In the distance, multiple sirens could be heard over the noise around them. Help was on the way.

"Kyle, there's another man," Ella shouted and grabbed his arm. Out of the corner of his eye, he saw a second man circling around the back of the vehicle. He whirled and fired before the man got off a shot, hitting him in the head. He dropped to the ground, lifeless.

As the patrol cars grew closer, the driver of the car must have realized they were outnumbered. He shoved the car in Drive and burned rubber as he flew from the parking lot.

Kyle leaped from behind the cover of the SUV and aimed at the retreating car. He couldn't let them get away. He'd gotten a good look at the driver and was almost positive it was Alhasan here in the United States. Everything he believed he knew about the terrorist had been turned on its ear. Nothing made sense.

The back window exploded and he could make out at least one man other than the driver as they whipped into traffic and sped through a red light, barely missing an oncoming car. Kyle mentally took down the license plate number, although he doubted it would help. The car was probably stolen.

With his pulse in panic mode, he hurried back to Ella. She'd risen from her hiding place and knelt next to the first man, securing his weapon. It was something he'd seen Lena do countless times as part of her training. Kyle felt for a pulse. It was weak and thready. He was fading quickly.

Kyle was reminded again how at times her behavior mirrored Lena's, but he wouldn't accept the possibility. He'd grieved for his wife for almost seven endless years. He'd been stuck in neutral, unable to move forward, still weighed down by the crushing loss.

"Are you okay?" he asked in a hard-edged tone invoked by his tormented memories. She slowly nodded. He checked the second man's pulse to be sure. There wasn't one.

He counted five patrol vehicles coming in hot as they surrounded them. The officers inside jumped from their cars with guns drawn.

"Drop your weapons now," one of them, who was dressed in a police chief's uniform, ordered.

Kyle immediately did as the chief requested. "Do what he says, Ella. They don't know what's happened here yet."

She tossed the weapon as far away from the injured man as possible.

Tracy and the pastor rushed down the steps to where Kyle and Ella stood.

"James, stay back," the chief warned.

The pastor didn't listen. "Henry, this man is the CIA agent I told you about. The woman is Ella Weiss, the former pastor's daughter. They didn't do anything wrong. Those men attacked them."

The chief sized Kyle and Ella up a second longer before he said, "Show me your ID."

Kyle slowly reached inside his pocket and produced the required identification and tossed it to the chief.

After careful scrutiny, the chief motioned to his men, who immediately lowered their weapons.

"Call for a bus," the chief ordered. "Looks like we have one severely injured and one dead." He then spoke to Kyle. "You want to tell me what's going on here, Agent Jennings?"

Kyle debated how much confidential information he should give away. Especially since Alhasan had proven he was more than capable of recruiting followers from all walks of life, even those sworn to protect, like his own team members who had betrayed them before. Abby had been a former Scorpion and she'd been persuaded to work for Alhasan.

Still, Kyle had a feeling he would need the chief's help to protect Ella. In his mind there was no choice.

He took the chief aside, out of Ella's hearing, to update the man briefly on what had taken place in Ella's past, with her being held captive and not remembering anything. He then gave him the car's description and the license plate number.

The chief motioned to one of his men. "Rick, get an APB out on the car, and you and your partner see if you can locate these guys. Take another patrol car with you. We don't want dangerous criminals running loose in our town."

"Yes, sir." The young officer hurried to fulfill the chief's command.

Kyle glanced at Ella. She looked as if she'd suffered a terrible shock and he had a feeling it was due to more than the firefight they'd just survived.

"Do you have a good description of this Alhasan person?" the chief asked Kyle.

"I do. I have a photo. I'll send it to your phone." The chief gave him the number and Kyle pulled up the photo of Alhasan.

Once the text went through, the chief said, "I'll get this out to all the local law enforcement agencies. If he shows his face anywhere around these parts, we'll nab him."

Kyle lowered his head to hide his misgivings. As much as he wished he could be as confident as the chief, he wasn't. "Alhasan is crafty. The CIA didn't nickname him the Fox without reason. He's managed to stay elusive for years. The fact that he's in the US is disturbing. Something is in play here that we don't fully understand yet. I appreciate your assistance on this, though. If we're done, I'd like to get Ella out of here. After what happened, this church is a little too public, and until we have Alhasan in custody and know the magnitude of what he has planned, he could have men watching us even now, waiting to strike again."

The chief nodded. "I think we're done. Might be a good idea to have a police escort out of here, though, just to make sure you're not followed."

While the chief was only trying to help, having a police escort out of town would be like a flashing neon sign calling attention to themselves unnecessarily. "Thanks for the offer, but I think we're better off on our own. I'm calling in my team for backup. If anything hinky comes up in the meantime, I'll let you know."

"If you're heading out of town, the best route is Highway 7. There's less traffic."

Kyle did a quick check on his phone's GPS. The route

was a little out of the way, but he could make it work. "That's fine."

"The offer stands if you need it. I'll call you when we have anything," the chief said.

The EMTs arrived and the chief walked over to speak with them.

Kyle went back to Ella's side. He considered how they were going to find another vehicle without raising suspicions.

"You can use my car," Tracy offered and held the key out to Kyle. "I have a spare at my house. It would be no trouble at all. I'd like to help Ella in any way I can," she added when Kyle hesitated. Tracy seemed innocent enough, and yet he knew better than to let his guard down for a minute.

"That's awfully kind of you, Tracy," he began, only to be interrupted by her.

"Agent Jennings, Ella's parents were good friends and I'm so happy to have her back home where she belongs. Her parents would have wanted me to help," she said with a watery smile.

He glanced at Ella and then asked, "Are you sure we're not inconveniencing you? You've been more than generous already."

Tracy shook her head. "No, not at all. It's the white one over there."

Kyle took the key and smiled gratefully. "Thanks for this."

Tracy nodded with tears in her eyes then stepped close to Ella and hugged her tight once more. "It's going to be okay. I promise you, everything will work out the way it's supposed to in time. If you do your part."

Ella jerked away as if the woman had struck her. She

stared at Tracy as if searching for some hidden meaning behind her words. He couldn't imagine how hard it must be for her to trust anyone, himself included. He knew she didn't like being touched. The scars on her body were evidence of horrible things she'd endured.

"Ready?" he asked, but she didn't answer. Together they walked in silence to the compact car close by.

Kyle wasn't about to let Ella out of sight. She was their only lead to Alhasan and his organization. While she didn't remember anything useful now, at some point she might be able to provide them with valuable information that would lead to his capture.

They drove through the light evening traffic until they reached the outskirts of town. It was up to him to keep her safe, and his hands tightened on the wheel. He hated working blindfolded without knowing what he was up against. The enemy could be anywhere, including... Kyle glanced Ella's way.

No, it couldn't be. Ella was the victim here, surely. She'd suffered so much. Her injuries weren't faked.

What about Stockholm syndrome?

It would certainly fit. Ella had been tortured and no doubt brainwashed enough to be a victim of Stockholm syndrome.

He shoved his doubts aside and did a quick check on the GPS to verify the correct turn was up ahead. The road was gravel and full of potholes and it seemed as if the weather had decided to play its part, as well. The snow came down harder now and he was no closer to having the answers he needed to protect Ella and hopefully save Sam and his team from certain death.

Kyle couldn't have felt more discouraged. As much

as he wanted to trust her fully, he couldn't. Not until he was certain where her allegiance stood.

He tried one more time to get through to her. "Ella, after what happened back there, you have to see they're coming after you full force. I need you to talk to me. I don't know what your reasons are for hesitating, but I want to try and understand. Help me, Ella. Help me save your life."

She stared straight ahead without answering and Kyle could no longer hide his frustration. He went for broke. "He'll keep coming. He won't stop until you're dead. Whoever you think you're protecting, it won't work."

She flinched and he realized he'd struck a nerve. "He's using them to gain your cooperation. Even if you do what he wants, he'll kill them and you. You can't trust him to keep his word." He stopped and added gently, "I know it's hard to tell the difference between the good guys and bad anymore, but I promise I'm one of the good guys. Tell me what he wants you to do, Ella. Who's the target?"

Her face crumpled at those words and tears she'd held back for so long flooded her eyes. "You are," she whispered through trembling lips. "You're the target, Kyle."

FOUR

Disbelief shot through his body like a bullet. Kyle wasn't sure he'd heard her correctly until he saw the anguish on her face. Nothing had prepared him for this. It felt as if the rug had been pulled out from under him and he struggled to wrap his head around what she'd said. He was the target? His first instinct was to say it was impossible, but a far more disturbing thought kept him quiet.

She'd drawn her weapon on him in the desert, her intentions unclear. She hadn't been honest with him from the beginning…and she'd been highly trained by someone. All things seemingly confirming his worst suspicions that Ella might be an enemy agent. He'd just never thought she was out for his blood.

She was clearly protecting someone close to her, which made her desperate, and desperate people could be talked into doing things they normally wouldn't consider.

Kyle forced his attention back to the road. "I think you'd better explain," he managed while trying to hold a steady tone.

Out of the corner of his eye he saw her run the heels of her hands over her eyes, but the tears wouldn't stop. It was as if a dam had broken somewhere down deep and her story of pain was finally unfolding.

"He told me he'd kept me alive for a reason," she said without emotion. "I had a job to do. As long as I did my part he'd…let me live." She'd hesitated just long enough for him to realize she wasn't telling the whole truth— and that was a huge problem. Sam and his team's chances of survival were slim at best, and Kyle was desperate to know why Alhasan was here in the United States.

"But I think it was all a lie," she continued.

Kyle swallowed his regret at what he had to do. She needed him to be strong, not to interrogate her. But *he* needed answers.

"It's okay, I know it's hard," he said. "What do you mean it was all a lie?"

The wariness in her eyes confirmed she still didn't fully trust him not to hurt her, and that was a bitter pill to swallow. He'd done all he could to convince her he was worthy. The rest was up to her.

"What does he want you to do, Ella?" he prompted.

She shifted in her seat so that she could look at him. "He wants me to integrate myself in with…you and then kill you."

Kyle couldn't make sense of it. Why did Alhasan want him dead so badly? Uneasiness rippled through him. "Why me specifically?" he asked and watched her shut down a little more. He was still working with half the puzzle.

"He just said you were part of the Scorpions and you needed to die." She stared straight ahead, her tone cool.

She knew about the Scorpion team. That would explain how she had his name. Seemed to recognize him.

"He told you about the Scorpions? What did he say?" Foolish question, but he wanted to hear what she knew.

"Just that they were CIA and had been in the way for a while." Still staring ahead, she fed him more half-truths. There was no way Alhasan would risk exposing his entire operation just to get back at Kyle. There was more to the story.

While his thoughts double-timed with possibilities, he realized he need to get word to his comrade Jase Bradford as soon as possible and tell him what he'd learned.

He glanced briefly at the woman by his side. He'd need to make the call without Ella listening in. As much as he wanted to trust her, with her still keeping secrets, he couldn't. Taking unnecessary risks wasn't an option.

"Is this the same man who took you?" he asked Ella.

Startled, she nodded. "Yes…at least I think he's the one who took me. He claims to be, but it's been so long and I was badly injured when I first arrived at the prison. I almost died. I've lost time. Memories. I'm not even sure I'm the person he told me I was."

That admission jerked his concentration to her once more. She wasn't sure she was Ella. He stuffed down the promise those words carried and asked, "What did he tell you about your past?"

"Just what you and I both know. That my name is Ella Weiss and that I was a missionary before I was captured…" Her wobbly voice trailed off. Emotionally shaken, it was a moment before she could go on. "He told me he killed the rest of my team and that he'd kept me alive for a purpose. But what if he lied about everything, Kyle? What if I'm not Ella Weiss at all? What if I'm really a killer?"

Her admission hit a little too close to his line of think-ing for comfort.

"Don't let him get in your head," Kyle told her. He couldn't imagine the things Alhasan would have said to convince her to do his bidding. He'd tried to break her physically and emotionally. He hadn't succeeded. The real woman was still in there, buried beneath years of pain.

Kyle glanced in the rearview mirror and spotted a car coming up quickly. He'd only seen their tire tracks behind him. No one else had been on the road recently and the car seemed to have come out of nowhere.

His fingers tensed on the wheel. Immediately, Ella picked up on his tension and glanced behind them.

"Do you think it's him?" Fear was laced through her tone.

As much as he would like to reassure her, he couldn't. "I don't know. Get down low so he doesn't see you. The sooner we get off this road and out of sight the better."

Still, Kyle couldn't afford to lead them to the lake house if they were being followed. He slowed so he could get a better view of the approaching vehicle. Nothing about it stood out as threatening, except the driver was going much too fast for the pitted road. As the car drew closer, Kyle noticed the man behind the wheel appeared to be the only one in the car.

The man honked several times in irritation at Kyle's slower speed, then roared into the oncoming lane and passed them, missing their car by inches. Kyle swerved toward the shoulder to prevent being sideswiped.

As the car sped by, he got a quick glimpse at the driver. His CIA training worked to his advantage, and through the dark and snowy conditions Kyle was able to see that the man appeared light-headed, and possibly mid- to late thirties. Nothing about him or the car sent any alarms up beyond the man's reckless driving.

"It's probably nothing more than an innocent traveler annoyed with our slow speed." His hopes at reassuring Ella failed miserably. As she sat up in the seat and turned toward him, he saw she was as white as a sheet.

When the car was completely out of sight, Kyle eased onto the gravel road that would take them to the lake house.

"We're almost there. That man may not be a threat, but we have no idea how many people Alhasan has working for him in the area."

She sucked in a breath. "How did you know his name?" She stared at him with the same distrust he'd seen in the desert.

He had to find a way to gain her trust. "My team has been watching him for years," he told her. "He's done some terrible things, Ella. He's taken lives. Hurt a lot of people. He has to be stopped." She shivered visibly at his ominous tone and suddenly stared at him as if she'd remembered something important.

"What is it?" he asked and prayed she would believe in him enough to confide.

"Nothing." She shook her head and turned away and he felt as if he'd lost a huge battle. What was it going to take to get her to have faith in him?

"Ella, you can trust me. I will protect you. I'll call in the rest of the team. They can be here by morning. We can take you someplace safe and out of Alhasan's reach."

She whirled on him with fresh terror in her eyes. "No. I don't want you to call them. You can't do that, Kyle."

He didn't understand her reluctance to have him bring in the team. "We can keep you safe—"

"I said no." She didn't let him finish. Yet it was his reaction that was most alarming. He didn't want her to walk away. "Why? Tell me that at least," he asked, trying to understand her reluctance.

As much as he hated working in the dark, right now she was the only lead he had to capturing Alhasan. He had to think about what was best for Sam and his men and let go of his personal feelings.

She shook her head. "If you call them in, I'm done co-operating. I'm serious, Kyle. I'll walk away and you'll never see me again."

"All right," he said at last and prayed his decision wouldn't cost more lives.

While Ella wanted to believe Kyle was one of the good guys, the stakes were too high for her to let down her guard even for a second.

Joseph was all she could think of. She was so afraid for the boy's safety. Why hadn't she just done what Alhasan wanted? Kyle had all but told her he would take her someplace safe, which could only mean the Scorpions' headquarters. She still had time to fulfill her mission.

Ella shook her head. The idea of taking Kyle's life filled her with sadness. She stuffed her hand over her mouth. She couldn't do it, because she felt something for him that was unexplainable.

She watched him squint through the falling snow as the path they were taking curved along the shores of Mountain Song Lake. For the moment, his full attention was on maneuvering the slick road and she could relax a little.

Once they reached the lake house, he'd be expecting more answers, and she had no idea what she was going to tell him. She struggled to come up with a plan. Was there still a chance she could convince Alhasan she would cooperate long enough to find out where he was holding Joseph?

With a drained sigh, she glanced out her window. There were only a handful of homes along this side of the lake. The road dead-ended past the last property. The lake house itself was secluded by trees and almost indiscernible from the road.

Kyle stopped the car out front. "This should be it," he said and surveyed the surrounding area with a frown. He was uneasy about the isolation. There would be limited means of escape should the enemy attack. How did she know that?

"If nothing else, there should be no reason for anyone to come this way by chance. I guess that's something." He turned to look at her. "Ready to go inside?"

Ella tried not to show her misgivings. She wasn't anywhere close to being ready. She was terrified of what she'd find. Or wouldn't. What if nothing about the place sparked a memory? Where did that leave her?

Kyle seemed to read all her uncertainties. "You'll know. One way or another, you'll know."

She smiled her gratitude and slowly nodded. "Yes, you're right."

He was being so protective of her even though she'd given him little to go on and no reason to believe her.

When he returned her smile, she found the confidence she needed to face what lay ahead.

"Good." He got out and came round to open her door.

Ella tried to control her fear-fueled breathing as they

stepped up on the porch together. Kyle slipped the key into the lock and opened the door. Once he went inside, he glanced back to her. It was her turn. She said a quick prayer for answers and then stepped over the threshold into a world she didn't know.

Kyle closed the door and dropped the bag containing her meager possessions—a change of clothes and some toiletries provided by the military—next to it.

Her hands actually shook. She was now only vaguely aware of Kyle as she moved to the compact living room and slowly looked around.

There were a couple of windows that would allow for a breathtaking view of the lake. A stone fireplace in the corner rose up to meet the ceiling. Wood was stacked on the floor next to it. The only pieces of furniture in the room were a worn caramel-colored leather sofa and an easy chair tucked close to the windows with a Bible lying open on the table close by.

She squeezed her eyes shut and tried to imagine the people who had once lived here. Her parents. Shouldn't she remember something about them by now? This was the house she'd grown up in. Surely she would recognize it if she really was who Alhasan told her she was.

Ella sensed Kyle watching her, waiting for some sign her memories had returned. How could she tell him nothing was farther from the truth?

She went over to the fireplace, where half a dozen pictures decorated the mantle. She recognized most of the people in them from the photo Tracy had given her. Moments in time captured at various stages of life. Marriage. The birth of their daughter. Ella as she grew into adulthood. Her high school and college graduations. Other pictures showed Ella with friends. Her years of captivity had changed her appearance drastically. She'd been through so much. She was drawn, her cheekbones hollow. Scarred physically and emotionally. She didn't even recognize that happy girl in the photos.

She glanced around the room. The people who once lived here didn't care much for material things. The heart of this house was the precious memoires captured in those photos.

Ella could no longer keep back her despair. Those memories were no clearer to her now than when she'd first looked at the photo. She dropped to her knees right there in front of the fireplace and covered her eyes with her hands. She hadn't felt this lost even in her prison cell. Part of her had always believed that once she and Joseph were free and safe, everything would fall into place. That, along with Joseph, had kept her fighting all these years.

Where did that leave her now?

Kyle knelt down beside her and gathered her in his arms. Her usual tense reaction to his closeness was there, but for once she needed the human contact to keep the darkness at bay. She clung to him and he held her tight.

"This isn't my life, Kyle. I'm not this person," she sobbed in a broken tone.

It was a long time before he answered, and during that space she wondered what he was thinking. "I know it's hard," he said quietly. "But you have to be patient. You've undergone years of brainwashing and pain. You've only been home for a day. It could take weeks if not longer before your memories fully return."

He was trying so hard to be strong for her, and yet there was something in his tone. Did he believe what he said? Fear crept up. What if she was a sleeper agent Alhasan had brainwashed into thinking she was Ella? What if the real Ella was dead?

"And if I never remember?" she asked in a shaken tone. The idea was terrifying. What if she had to live in this limbo for the rest of her life? How could she possibly exist?

Kyle stroked a thumb across her cheek and she glanced up at him. The strength she saw in his eyes reached down deep inside her and chipped away at the distrust that had become part of her.

"You will. All you need is time and rest. Once you've healed physically and emotionally, your memories will return. I'm positive of it," he said with a tender smile.

She wished she could be so certain, but Kyle had enough faith for the both of them. He was a good man. She touched a strand of his chestnut-brown hair and a sense of recognition shot through her. He wore it longer now.

How would she know that?

Ella sucked in a breath and scanned his handsome face as if searching for answers. Why did Kyle seem so familiar? It didn't make sense. They'd never met before. Was it just her mind latching onto the details Alhasan had told her about Kyle?

His smile suddenly evaporated, his eyes clouding with some unknown emotion. As they continued to stare at each other, just the faintest of recollections tormented her with uncertainty. He'd looked at her with that same expression once before. Her brows knit together, trying to understand what she was remembering.

"What is it?" he asked when she couldn't cover her perplexity. She couldn't begin to explain why he was the only familiar thing in her world.

"Ella?" he prompted when she didn't answer.

She shook her head. "Nothing. It's nothing. I'm just tired, I guess."

Sadness replaced the curiosity she'd seen in him moments earlier. She wasn't being truthful and he knew it.

"Why don't you stretch out for a bit?" he said and let her go.

This wasn't what she wanted. She wanted…well, she wasn't really sure what she wanted, only that being with Kyle made her wish for things she couldn't remember thinking about in the past. If she were truly Ella Weiss, then she had been in love once. Her fiancé, David, had proposed to her and they'd been engaged to be married. What had she felt back then? Had she been excited for their future together?

"You're right. I think I will lie down," she managed.

Kyle got to his feet and drew her up, as well. "I'm not sure which room was yours before, but the one just down the hall and on the ground floor is the safest." She knew what he meant. It would be easy to escape should someone come after them.

He grabbed her bag and headed that way. She slowly followed like a robot empty of emotion.

Kyle deposited her bag next to the door and faced her. "Try to sleep, Ella. You'll be surprised how much clearer things will appear once you're rested." He looked deep into her eyes and soon the tenderness she saw in him shifted to other wishes. He stepped closer, a mere whisper away, and she shuddered. She'd endured years of being hurt. She'd forgotten what it felt like to be handled tenderly like Kyle was doing now.

Her eyes drifted closed. Seconds ticked by and then he brushed her hair from her face and pressed his lips against her forehead. Her eyes flew open. She recognized the gesture. She remembered it from… She couldn't grasp the memory, and she'd never felt so frustrated.

"I'm going to take a look around the area. Check things out. I'll lock the door behind me just to be careful. Good night, Ella," he said and turned and left before she could answer.

Was it just her imagination or was there just a touch of regret in his tone?

FIVE

Kyle walked out the door like a man who had suffered a tremendous jolt. His intentions had started out good. She was upset; he wanted to comfort her. Yet the result had been unplanned and had ended in a kiss. He'd let his emotions win out. He couldn't afford to do that if he wanted to keep her safe.

Ella had been distraught. Confused by what was happening. He was positive she hadn't recognized anything about the house or the family photos, and it didn't make sense. He'd thought once she was in her childhood home, some of her past would return.

She was so much like Lena. Their voices were almost identical, and every second he spent with Ella reinforced the likeness. Yet there were differences beyond the length of her hair. Emotional differences he couldn't relate to his wife. Ella was filled with fear and distrust. Her insecurities evident. Lena never doubted herself.

Still, he wondered what Lena would be like if she'd suffered the things Ella had.

Kyle recalled his earlier conversation with Tracy, the outcome of which had been unexpected. When he'd pressed Tracy for something of Ella's that might contain

DNA evidence for testing, she'd gotten defensive. He partly understood. After all, the woman had just identified Ella and he was demanding more proof. Still, without concrete evidence, the question about her true identity would always haunt him. He couldn't get the resemblance to his dead wife out of his head and wouldn't allow himself to get his hopes up without something more solid.

Now more than ever, he needed grounding. A friendly voice to tell him what he was thinking was way off base. Jase Bradford was one of the best agents Kyle had ever had the privilege of training. They'd grown close through their years of working together. He trusted Jase implicitly and he'd hand picked him to head the Scorpion team.

Jase was only person he counted on to steer him in the right direction. He'd texted Jase earlier, when they first reached the house, with the license plate number and the information Ella had told Kyle about him being Alhasan's target.

This time he'd call.

"Buddy, I'm glad you called. I have the info on the plate. Looks like it belongs to a man by the name of Peter Duncan. The address is 907 Laurel Lane, right there in Mountain Song."

Kyle typed the address into Google Maps. "It's here on the lake." An awfully big coincidence.

"I don't think I buy this is all just a fluke," Jase said in an ominous tone. "I'll do some checking on Duncan. See what I can find out about his past. In the meantime, keep your eyes open for him."

"I will. Maybe I'm being paranoid. Seeing problems that don't exist."

"After what happened today at the church, I'd say you have good reason to be cautious," Jase assured him.

Kyle managed a laugh. It was good hearing his friend's voice after everything that happened since the desert. "You're right. That was a bit hairy."

"How are things there? Any progress with Ella?" Jase asked as if sensing he needed to talk. Kyle closed his eyes. So far, nothing that was happening with Ella or the assault in town made sense, and he'd lost his ability to analyze the situation clearly.

He explained how Ella refused to let him call in the team. Jase's silence told him that didn't sit well. "I'd be curious to know why she doesn't want us involved."

"I wish I knew," Kyle said wearily. He told Jase about Ella not recognizing Tracy or her own family home. "What do you make of it?" he asked, because he needed Jase's opinion. The man had worked closely with Lena before her death.

The amount of time it took for Jase to respond promised an unwelcome answer.

"I know I don't have to tell you this, but you have to be very careful. I see it, too, Kyle. The photo you sent of her while you were at Bagram, well, her resemblance to Lena is unsettling, to say the least. Which is all the more reason you have to protect yourself. I know how much you hurt when you lost Lena. I don't want you to have to go through that again." Jase paused a second longer and then confirmed Kyle's greatest fears. "You have to accept the fact that she could have been groomed for use by Alhasan simply because she does resemble Lena."

Kyle understood exactly what Jase meant. Losing his wife had pretty much crippled him. If he hadn't turned to God and had his faith to lean on, he wasn't sure he would have made it through.

"I know, but it's so hard. Being near her. Seeing Lena

in some of her gestures…" He stopped and glanced around at the moonless night. But she wasn't Lena and that was the hard part. Everything about her reminded him of what he'd lost.

As always, Jase had his back. "I can't even imagine. All the more reason to be cautious." Jase was only trying to protect him, but following that advice was getting harder to do.

"I've tried contacting Liz, but she's not answering. Have you heard anything from her yet?" Jase asked.

As happy as he was to change the subject, it had now been almost forty-eight hours since he'd last spoken to his second in command. He'd talked with Alex Booth, who had filled him in on what happened. She and Michael had been chasing down a location they believed might lead to where the hostages were being held. When they didn't check in after a few hours, Booth had ordered a search party to be dispatched with him and Dalton leading the team. Kyle told Jase what he'd found out.

"I don't like it. It isn't like Liz not to check in." Jase said, his fears mirroring Kyle's.

"You're right." It was as if they'd disappeared into thin air. "Hopefully, we'll have good news soon," Kyle said and wished he felt as positive.

"Let's hope. I'll let you know what I find out about Duncan." Jase paused a second and then added, "I'm praying for you and so is Reyna."

Kyle was humbled by his friend's concern. Although he and Reyna had only known each other for a short time, he felt as if Jase's wife was a good friend already.

"Thanks. Tell Reyna the same. In my book you can never have enough prayers."

Jase chuckled. "You got that right. 'Night, buddy. Stay

safe. If you need our help, don't hesitate, no matter the time."

Kyle ended the call without any real sense of peace and took stock of his surroundings. On the other side of the lake, only a single house was lit up. It had been dark when they'd arrived. He had no idea how many others were across the way.

They'd passed three homes on the road leading to the lake house. All appeared empty. Tracy had told him there were lots of vacation homes up here so it stood to reason not too many would be occupied full-time.

Still, his training had him going over an exit strategy in his head. With no other houses past theirs, the only feasible way out without a vehicle would be on foot. If someone ventured this way, there would be no retracing their steps to the main road. The lake appeared to be more than half a mile across. Swimming it would be a near-impossible feat in Ella's physical condition and with the December cold. Hypothermia would set in within minutes.

He glanced back at the house. He'd closed all the blinds and had kept the lights off, so it was dark inside. He'd give anything to understand this pull she had on him beyond her physical resemblance to Lena. If felt as if there was a connection between them that defied explanation.

Had he lied when he told her everything would be better when she was rested? What if she woke up and remembered everything about her life as Ella? What if she didn't?

Kyle wasn't sure which he hoped for anymore. Throughout the long, lonely years while he'd grieved for his wife, he'd also had a sense of something left unfinished with Lena's death that couldn't be explained. He'd always assumed it had something to do with the argument they'd had before she left for that final mission. But what if it was more?

Foolish. He had to let go of those thoughts and stay focused.

He made his way down the short path to the shore. There was a boat dock close by that he assumed the neighboring houses shared, yet no boats were secured there.

Kyle returned to the car and pulled out the night-vision binoculars he'd stashed in his bag and focused them across the lake. There appeared to be four houses there. All but the one were dark. He homed in on the illuminated one and its surrounding area. The same car that had passed them earlier was parked outside. Duncan. The address would match the one Jase gave him. Still, an uneasy feeling settled into the pit of his stomach. He fought the instinct to rush back to the house, wake Ella and get out of there. With everything that happened in town and the realization that Alhasan was here in the same area, Jase was right. The odds were just too much to ignore.

He zeroed in on the rooms that were lit. Several blinds were open. He could see the living and dining areas. Nothing inside stood out as the lair of a terrorist. Still, he didn't like it.

As an added precaution, Kyle pulled the car around to the back of the house as close to it as he dared. There was a small storage shed tucked in close to the tree line. Inside, he found an aluminum fishing boat and oars. Not the easiest way to cross, but if they had to, they could make it to the other side.

He took the boat to the dock and tied it off, then he did

a quick search around the home's exterior. Nothing appeared out of place, so he went back inside. Sleep wasn't going to be an option for him. He went to Ella's room and cracked the door open. She lay on her left side, facing away from the room's entrance. She didn't stir. She had both hands tucked beneath her cheek. Exactly like Lena used to do.

Kyle closed the door and went back to the living room. With so many things about her reminding him of his late wife, he couldn't help but wonder: If she was Lena, then why couldn't she remember *him*?

His emotions were in shreds. He knelt next to the sofa and prayed. Now more than ever he was desperate for God's strength.

Kyle poured out his heart and felt the welcomed peace that came from turning all his troubles over to God.

A quick check of his watch confirmed it was just after midnight. With Sam's survival chances dwindling as each second ticked past, Kyle tried to reach Liz once more. The call went straight to voice mail. A call to Michael produced the same results. Liz was his lifeline on the ground in Afghanistan. He didn't believe she would willingly turn off her phone.

He'd give it an hour and try again, and if she still didn't answer he'd call Booth for an update. He wouldn't wait any longer, because his gut was warning him a terrible thing had happened out there in the desert.

Something woke her. Ella sat up quickly and listened, her heart pounding, her survival instincts keen. As she started to get up, she felt the soft bed beneath her fingers. She wasn't in the torture zone any longer. She was safe.

She struggled to calm her nerves. Would there ever

come a time when she'd truly be free of the nightmare? She was thousands of miles away and yet she felt as if she were still a prisoner.

Light filtered through curtained windows. It was morning. She'd slept through the night for the first time in years.

Then she realized what had woken her. Voices. Ella swung her legs off the bed and stood. Her body ached from years of abuse.

She slipped out of the room and followed the voices. The front door stood ajar. Kyle was talking to someone. Another man, but she really couldn't make out the voice.

Kyle turned when she came into the room. When he spotted her, something in his expression warned her to stay put. She moved back into the shadows of the hallway and listened.

"Well, thanks for stopping by, Mr. Duncan."

The other man said something indistinguishable.

"No problem." Kyle's tone was noticeably tense. He held up what looked like a business card. "I have your card and I will."

After the two men shook hands, Kyle closed the door and faced her. To say he was worried would be an understatement.

"Who was that?" she prompted, because his expression scared her.

"The man in the car who almost ran us off the road yesterday. Believe it or not, he lives across the lake."

She tried to make sense of it. "How did he find us?"

Kyle went over to the window and inched the curtains apart. Ella followed. She could only see the back of the man as he walked away. He had blond hair...*just like the American at the prison.*

"He said he walks around the lake every morning and he spotted our car and felt bad about yesterday. He wanted to apologize."

This was no accidental meeting. If this was the American from the prison, then things were much worse than she thought. He would know she was here with Kyle and would be expecting results.

"But you don't believe it," she managed.

He seemed to be debating how much to tell her. "No, I don't. I spoke to one of my team members last night. He told me the man's name is Peter Duncan." Kyle shook his head. "Then, in a text this morning, I found out Duncan and his wife have lived here for over six years. He's an accountant and she works at a shop in the neighboring town of Brenton. There's nothing that triggers any warning other than the fact that he was on the same road as us and he found us here."

"Why would he come all the way over here just to apologize to people he doesn't know?"

She could tell from the hard set of Kyle's jaw that he agreed there was reason for concern. "Maybe he really is just a nice guy who felt bad about losing his temper yesterday."

Her gaze held his. "You don't believe that." It wasn't a question.

"Not really. After what happened in town and in light of some of the intel we've received recently, we believe Alhasan could have men everywhere. Sleepers ready to do his bidding."

Was she one of them? When her memories finally returned would she find out she really was a killer?

Please, God, no.

She recalled something Alhasan had told her about

moving his entire operation to the United States. He'd said there were too many people in Afghanistan looking to gain the reward being offered by the Scorpions for his capture. He couldn't trust them not to turn him in. And the American was growing impatient. Something critical was in the works.

He wanted her to gain access to the Scorpions' headquarters for a reason… She closed her eyes and tried to hold on to it. He needed something hidden there, but she couldn't recall what it was.

Once, she'd pretended to be unconscious and overhead the American discussing her with Alhasan. He'd shown doubts about her ability to fulfill her mission from the beginning. He'd said she had too much of a personal stake involved to finish the job. She had no idea what he meant by that. Was it simply because of her attachment to Joseph?

"What is it?" Kyle asked when he spotted her reaction. "Have you remembered something?"

Would she be giving away too much if she told him what she suspected? Joseph's image popped into her head. She still had a few days left to save him. She couldn't do anything that might cost the boy his life.

She shook her head and started to move away.

"Ella…" He came closer, preventing her from escaping. Clasping her chin gently, he tipped her head back so that she was forced to look into his eyes. She struggled not to jerk away. The same warmth his touch had invoked before returned. "You can tell me, whatever it is."

If only it were that simple.

When she didn't answer, he dropped his hand and his tone turned hard. "I need you to stay here and lock the door behind me. I should be back within the hour." He took out his spare Glock and handed it to her along with a burner phone. "If anything comes up, call me. If someone tries to break in, shoot them."

"Where are you going?" she asked in fear. He was leaving her here alone.

He checked his watch. "It's almost nine. I'm going to wait for Peter Duncan to leave for work, and then I'm going to see what I can find out about the man by searching his house."

She grabbed his arm and stood her ground. "I'm coming with you."

"No, Ella, it's too dangerous. Alhasan wants you dead. Duncan could be working for him."

She shook her head. "You're the target, Kyle. He couldn't care less about me as long as I…" She broke off. She'd almost told him everything.

Kyle stilled. "As long as you what?"

She didn't answer. "I'm coming with you," she insisted and squared her shoulders, ready to battle him. "I can help. I know what to look for…" Her voice trailed off. How did she know?

Frustration claimed its rightful place next to his growing curiosity, yet he finally gave in. "All right, but you stay close."

Kyle went to the back of the house and cracked the door. She followed. After a quick surveillance of the area, he stepped outside. "We'll have to circle around the lake through there." He pointed to a wooded area overgrown with brush and trees. "If he's watching the house still, he won't be able to see us here."

Nothing about the thicket looked inviting, but she wasn't about to give in to her paranoia. If Alhasan was close by, then there was the chance Joseph might be with him. She'd risk her life to save the boy.

Kyle stopped in front of the overrun opening leading into the woods. After a second when he appeared to close his eyes and pray, he shoved aside some of the tree branches and headed in with her close behind.

Within no time the rigorousness of the trail took its toll and she found herself winded. After they fought their way at a snail's pace through branches snagging their clothes and ripping their exposed skin, the path finally dumped them out of the woods and into an open area.

Ella was so exhausted she didn't think she could make it much farther. She sucked in a lungful of air and noticed that Kyle looked worried.

"Try slowing your breathing down," he suggested as he watched her struggle to do so. "We need to hide. If Duncan's watching, he might see and be expecting us."

Speaking was out of the question, so she nodded. Kyle pointed to the closest house. "There's a shed over there. That should give us some cover."

Once she reached the shed, Ella braced her hands against her knees and closed her eyes.

"You're ready to drop. Wait here and keep a watch out for anyone coming up to the house."

She immediately rejected the idea and straightened. There was too much at stake. Joseph might be in the house. "I'll be fine. I'm just a little winded. I'm going with you, Kyle."

His misgivings were obvious. "Stay behind me, and if you feel yourself struggling, I need you to let me know."

Kyle eased to the back of the shed and pulled out a small set of binoculars. He panned the area and then said, "I have the house. The car's still there… Hang on, it looks like he's leaving."

He handed her the binoculars and she saw Duncan get into his car and slowly back out of the drive. He had the basic build and look of the American, but she wasn't sure.

Once the car was out of sight, Kyle took the binoculars and tucked them back in his pocket, shoving the Glock at his waist underneath his jacket.

As they headed down the road toward Duncan's place, she felt exposed like she had in the desert. They passed several clearly empty houses showing no signs of life inside. Either the occupants were at work or these were vacation homes.

Once they reached the front of Duncan's house, Kyle did a quick check around. "I don't think anyone's watching. Let's do this quickly."

They hurried to the back. "Check the windows. We need a way inside and we can't afford to break in. I don't want him knowing we were here." Kyle tried the back door. It was locked.

Ella tried several windows with the same results.

"Over here," Kyle said as he slid one of windows open. "Let me go in first and make sure everything's okay. I'll let you in the back door."

She waited while he eased through the opening. With her nerves shot, she was jumping at every noise and it seemed to take forever before Kyle opened the door.

"I checked around to make sure the house was empty. According to my intel, the wife leaves for work around seven each morning. Still, we don't know how much time we have so we need to search the house as quickly as possible. I'll take the top floor. Can you handle down here?"

It surprised her how easily they worked together. Almost as if they'd done this same thing before… She shook her head. Preposterous. The chances of them having met before were slim. There would be no reason for them to have worked together.

"You're looking for anything that doesn't fit with your everyday Joe. If you're not sure, let me see it. If you hear anything suspicious, come get me."

She nodded and he hurried upstairs while Ella began searching the living room. There were photos of the couple together. Most appeared staged and a little too perfect to be realistic. Nothing from vacations taken together or family gatherings. She stared closely at the man in the photo. Could he be the same American from the prison?

Ella spotted a desk in the corner of the room. Mail had been piled high on it. She examined it closer. Most of it appeared to be bills, and all were addressed to Peter Duncan. Nothing for the wife.

A quick search of the drawers produced only a handful of pens. Other than the staged photos and the bills, the room contained nothing personal. No books or movies. Not even a newspaper to make the house seem as if it were actually being lived in and wasn't just a front.

Ella checked the downstairs bedrooms and bath, and found more of the same. The closet in the master bedroom held only a couple of items of men's clothing. Was the wife nothing more than a cover?

She started for the kitchen when she noticed another door hidden beneath the staircase. She tried opening it, but it was locked. Why was the door locked? Her first thought was Joseph. Was he being held there? Ella felt around the top of the door frame until she located a key. That was a little too easy to find. Would she be walking into a trap?

She slowly opened the door. No sound could be heard from inside. She flipped on the lights and charged down the stairs. The room was dank and cobwebs hung from all the corners. Dust covered the few items in the space. There was no sign of Joseph or any evidence that anyone had used the basement in a long time.

Her spirits sank. For a moment, she'd hoped—even though she knew Alhasan well enough to know he wouldn't make it that easy.

Where could Alhasan have him stashed? She needed some clue if she had any chance of saving Joseph. The child's time was running out.

She returned to search the kitchen, which provided only more dead ends. The usual pots and pans, a drawer full of old batteries, the bare minimum of food in the fridge and pantry. Nothing that indicated someone spent a lot of time and prepared meals here. With unanswered questions flying through her head, Ella continued her search. She couldn't give up now.

Inside a drawer near the sink, something captured her attention. It was a piece of paper stuck in the back of an old cookbook. The paper was a receipt from three years ago. It was from an airport restaurant in Kabul. Kyle had told her Duncan lived here with his wife for six years, so she concluded the receipt had to be Duncan's. But what was an accountant doing in Kabul, Afghanistan?

Before she could process it, a sound from outside captured her attention. She listened carefully. It came from the front of the house, where she'd just been. A board creaking under someone's footsteps.

Ella stuffed the receipt in her pocket, headed for the stairs just as Kyle descended them. She put her finger up to her lips and pointed to the front.

He nodded and reached her side as a key slipped in the door. He pointed toward the back and she understood. Their only means of escape was quickly evaporating. Before they managed even a single step, a figure of a man stepped up on the back porch and spotted them.

He shoved through the door at the same time the front entrance was breached and they came face-to-face with Peter Duncan. But it was the second man who captured Ella's attention—the man who had attacked her at the base.

Both were armed with guns.

Kyle pushed Ella behind him, whipped out his Glock and pointed it at Duncan's head. The man stopped dead in his tracks.

Her attacker smiled a sinister grin. "You should have listened, Ella. Done what you were supposed to do. Instead you fell in with the enemy. Now you'll die with him. I guess we'll have to take care of the rest of them ourselves…along with the boy."

Her stomach clenched in fear. Joseph.

"Tell your guy to drop his weapon, Duncan. Or you'll be dead before he can get off a single shot," Kyle ordered in the same steely tone she'd heard him use in the desert.

Duncan didn't react. "And my partner will take you both out. He's very well trained, thanks to your people." The jab didn't go undetected. The implication was clear. The man who attacked her had US military training.

They needed an advantage and quickly. If she could reach the Glock tucked behind her back, she was positive she could take out her attacker. At least eliminate part of the threat.

She slowly eased her hand behind her body. Kyle must

have realized what she was doing, because he turned just a smidgen, partially blocking her from Duncan's partner.

"You're not going to hurt her," Kyle said, trying to call their bluff. "She's too important to your cause."

Duncan laughed as if enjoying the exchange. "You think you know what's happening here, Agent Jennings?" He shook his head. "You have no idea."

Kyle tapped her arm twice. She recognized the signal somehow.

Ella whipped the weapon out and fired once, hitting her attacker between the eyes. He dropped to the floor, dead. Before a stunned Duncan had time to react, Kyle opened fire. Duncan dived for cover, racking off multiple shots in the process. Kyle grabbed Ella's arm and they raced for the cover of the kitchen island.

"Do your part, Ella. There's still time to save the boy."

She squeezed her eyes shut. Duncan was trying to use Joseph's life as a bargaining chip.

Kyle touched her arm and she looked at him. "We're going through there," he whispered and pointed to the side window. "I'll cover you. When you're free, start running and don't look back."

Ella didn't budge. She wasn't about to leave him. "I'm not going without you. You never leave a man behind."

He smiled at her valor and scrubbed a thumb across her cheek. Her eyes closed briefly, and she swallowed involuntarily in reaction.

"I'll be right behind you," he assured her in a gravelly voice—its familiarity seemed to reach out and grab her from the past.

"You'll only have a second. Ready?" She wasn't, but she had a job to do. She nodded. "On three."

Her heart pounded in her ears as he counted off. On

the three count, Kyle shot the window and glass shattered everywhere, then he leaped to his feet and opened fire. Duncan quickly returned it.

Ella kept as low as she could and slipped through the broken window. The second she cleared the deck, she ran for her life. Once she reached the opening to the woods, she paused to listen. She wasn't leaving Kyle behind. She'd wait. If he didn't come soon, she'd go back for him.

A handful of seconds ticked by before she spotted him. He caught up with her quickly enough.

"We have to hurry. I don't doubt he'll come after us," he assured her and grabbed her hand as they raced through the woods at a frantic pace. Once they'd covered some distance from the house, Kyle stopped and she turned to him.

"What is it?" she asked because she didn't like the look on his face.

"I need you to keep going, Ella. Don't stop," he said in a tone that sent chills through her. "No matter what happens, don't stop."

SIX

She shook her head. "No, Kyle, I'm not leaving without you."

The crunch of undergrowth beneath a footstep drew his attention behind them. Duncan was coming after them.

He knew Ella heard it, too. She whipped around. "He's right behind us." The fear in her voice was evident in every syllable.

He didn't bother looking behind them. "Keep moving and don't stop. I'm going to draw his attention in another direction."

She grabbed his arm. "He has nothing to lose. He'll kill you."

"I'll be okay," he said with assurance. "Just keep going the same direction we came. When you clear the woods, stay out of sight and wait for me. If I'm not back soon, get to the car and go into town. Find the chief. He can help you." When she hesitated, he gave her a gentle nudge. "Go, Ella. He's almost here."

With a final searching look, she did as he asked and turned and ran down the path. Once more, Kyle was struck by how closely she resembled Lena. The way she carried herself. Her body language. Her instant ability to interpret his signal earlier. Even the way she ran. If they survived this, he'd have to find a way to positively identify her as Ella Weiss. Because his heart couldn't take another crushing blow like he'd experienced with Lena's death.

Kyle shoved his personal feelings down deep and found adequate cover. He listened as Duncan's steps slowed. The man must suspect Kyle was planning something. Still, Kyle held his position. If his idea worked, Duncan would hear Ella and go after her. He'd walk straight into the trap.

A dozen or more seconds ticked by before Duncan finally emerged from his cover. Kyle waited until he was past him before he stepped out with weapon drawn.

"That's far enough."

The man stopped dead in his tracks then slowly turned and faced Kyle. "Nicely played, Agent Jennings. Too bad she'll be dead before she reaches the car."

Nothing showed on Duncan's face. Kyle prayed it was a bluff. "You're lying."

"Am I?" Duncan challenged. "Are you willing to stake her life on it?"

Kyle didn't take the bait. "You're going to tell me where Alhasan is and what he has planned."

Duncan laughed as if Kyle had said something amusing. "You're kidding. You have no idea the scope of this operation. Who the real enemy is. You think she's on your side." He added the jab slowly and then grinned.

The man was trying to get under his skin, and it was working. Kyle kept the Glock trained on Duncan's head and grabbed his phone. He'd take Duncan in. Once he had Ella stashed someplace safe, he'd interrogate the man himself.

Duncan realized what he was planning and dived for the gun. Kyle leaped out of the way before he could grab the weapon. The move gave Duncan enough time to scramble for tree coverage.

Kyle quickly did the same. "Give yourself up, Duncan. It's over."

The man's answer was to open fire. A round of bullets hit the tree Kyle was standing behind. He peered around and another round of shots sped past his head, forcing him to duck. A few seconds later, he could hear Duncan heading back in the direction of the house.

Kyle jumped from behind his cover and opened fire while Duncan zigzagged between trees, making it impossible to get a clear shot. When Duncan popped into view, Kyle aimed at his right side and fired.

One of the rounds hit and the man screeched in pain. For a second Kyle thought he was going down. He stumbled a couple of steps then got his legs beneath him once more.

Kyle gave chase, but with Duncan firing over his shoulder, he was forced to take cover once more.

As much as Kyle wanted to bring Duncan in, he wasn't willing to take the chance. What if his threats were real? He needed to get Ella out of there quickly, because every second Alhasan knew her whereabouts meant she was in danger.

Her labored breathing echoed in her ears, drowning out all other sound—yet she didn't dare stop. Ella kept running, shoving branches out of her way, all the while praying for Kyle's safety. She couldn't bear it if anything happened to him. She wasn't sure when it'd happened, but she realized now that he was all she had to hold on to without Joseph.

When she reached the edge of the woods, out of breath and close to fainting, Ella was forced to stop. She leaned her hands against her knees and listened. The eerie silence behind her was broken by a rapid exchange of gunfire.

Ella clamped her hand over her mouth.

Please keep him safe. She said the frantic prayer in her head as the sporadic shooting continued. Then silence, soon followed by a car firing in the distance. Tires protesting on gravel as the vehicle flew down a road.

She turned and ran back into the woods at a frantic pace and almost slammed into Kyle.

Relief threatened to buckle her knees. Without thinking, she threw her arms around him and held on tight.

"I heard shots. Are you okay?" she asked when her heartbeat slowed and she could actually manage words.

Kyle stiffened for a second then gathered her close. "I'm okay. He got away, but he's injured."

If Duncan really was the American, would he follow through with his threat against Joseph? The thought was terrifying.

"We can't go back to the lake house," Kyle told her in a terse voice. "We need help, Ella. Duncan could have called in backup. We're at a disadvantage. You have to let me call in—"

"No." She didn't let him finish. "You can't call in the Scorpions. He'll kill Joseph." She pulled away and put space between them.

He stared at her, his frustration evident. "What are you talking about? Who's Joseph?" When she didn't answer, he stepped in front of her and forced her to look at him. "You have to be honest with me, Ella. The time for keeping secrets is over. What haven't you told me?"

He was trying to save her life. She saw that now. As hard as it was to trust anyone not to hurt her again, she really believed Kyle was one of the good guys. He'd proven it to her over and over again.

"Joseph is just a little boy," she said in a strangled voice. "He's so innocent and I can't bear the thought of anything happening to him. Kyle, I have to protect him."

She watched anger flare in his eyes. "A child? How do you know him?"

Ella let out an unsteady breath. "Because he was with me at the prison."

"The boy was being held as a prisoner?" He couldn't disguise his disgust. "What about his parents?"

She shook her head. "I don't know." She remembered the woman. Alhasan's bragging.

"Ella, please, I need you to tell me why you don't want me to call in my team. Is it because of the boy?"

She wanted to trust him with everything, but Joseph's life was on the line. She shook her head.

"Then at least let me reach out to the chief. Have him pick us up and get us safely out of here. We can't go back for the car, and Duncan knows we're here."

There had been no sign of Joseph at the house, but Duncan had mentioned they'd keep him alive if she followed through with the plan. Was there a way to convince him she would do as he asked? What if the police chief was part of Alhasan's team? Uncertainty swirled around in her head.

"What if the chief is working for Alhasan?" She voiced her fears aloud. "He has men everywhere."

"That's the very reason we can't keep going alone," he said calmly. "We're fighting an enemy who could be right next to us. I trust the chief. You can, too."

"Okay," she said at last and hoped she hadn't sealed Joseph's fate once and for all.

SEVEN

"With the exception of my wife, no one knows about this place. Not even my men. You should be safe here," the chief assured Kyle. "Molly and I come here from time to time to get away from things. Mostly when my job gets to be too much."

"We're thankful for your help, Chief," Kyle said with gratitude.

"It's Henry, and you're both welcome."

Kyle glanced curiously at the man seated next to him. He'd told Ella he trusted Henry because he needed to keep her moving, yet with everything that had happened, he was starting to second-guess the wisdom of calling the man. For the moment, his hands were tied. Henry seemed solid enough, but then again, Alhasan had proven he could convince the most dedicated people to do his bidding if he put enough pressure on them or dangled enough money.

In the backseat, Ella was huddled with her arms wrapped tight around her body. The same protective posture he'd seen her in a few times. She trusted no one. Not even him. After what she'd been through, he could certainly understand, but at some point the only way to move forward was to reach out to someone for help.

"I take it your wife isn't a fan of your job?" Kyle asked Henry, making Ella glance up from her musing. Their gazes tangled. Awareness sparked in hers. She remembered something.

Henry laughed. "You could say that. Molly and I have been married for going on thirty years now and I've been on the force through all of them."

Kyle noticed Ella was listening intently. Something about Henry's story grabbed her attention.

"That's an amazing career," Kyle said. He'd give just about anything to know what had her so curious.

Henry nodded. "But not without its price. I've been shot at—" he pointed to his left shoulder "—stabbed and I came close to being blown up once. Still, I wouldn't trade a minute of it." He spared Kyle a knowing look. "It's hard on the people we love, though. They have to pay the price in sleepless nights and days spent worrying we won't come home."

Like Lena. A lump formed in Kyle's throat that he couldn't clear away. He'd gone out of his mind worrying about her on that final mission, and his worst nightmare had become a reality.

He noticed Ella's eyes filled with tears and she looked away. What was she thinking about?

"Anyway, I promised Molly after I survived the shooting last spring this was it. My last year of wearing a badge, and I aim to keep that vow. I'm retiring at the end of the month. Then we're going to move to our little cabin and I'm going to do my best to not worry Molly ever again."

Kyle hadn't really ever thought about the future until

he lost Lena. He'd always assumed they would grow old together.

He'd give just about anything to turn back time. Change the past. Be the man she'd needed him to be.

Henry slowed the car's speed and then turned onto a gravel drive. After they'd traveled close to a quarter of a mile, he stopped in front of a two-story log cabin tucked deep in the woods. Snow still clung to the eaves and most of the surrounding trees. A perfect hideaway.

"The wife and I come out here most weekends, so there's food and necessities," Henry told them as he got out, and Kyle and Ella followed. "We keep some clothes here, as well. Not sure if any of it will fit you, Ella. My wife's a bit petite, but you're welcome to try."

"Thank you," she said as she stepped inside the cabin, followed by Kyle. Henry flipped on the lights and Kyle got a good look at the place.

It reminded him of the cabin where he and Lena spent their honeymoon in Montana. Memories washed over him. Their time together had been so special. If only he'd known how little of it they had.

Ella made the tiniest of sounds. He turned and realized something was wrong. She looked as if she'd suffered a terrible shock. His heart belted out a crazy tune. Had she remembered something from her past?

"Agent Jennings?" Kyle became aware of Henry saying something to him and he had no idea what.

"Sorry," he apologized. "I was thinking about something else."

Henry looked at him funny but let the matter go. "If you need anything, call me and I can be here in ten minutes."

"I will. Thanks, Henry." Kyle shook the man's hand.

"You're welcome." He nodded to Ella. "I'll let you two get settled in. Treat it like you own it," he said with a final wave.

Before Henry left there was something Kyle needed to ask him in private.

"I'll be right back," he told Ella and followed the man outside to his car.

"Something on your mind, Agent Jennings?" Henry asked once they were out of earshot.

Kyle got straight to the point. "There is. I need a favor."

Henry never wavered. "Name it."

"I'm having trouble finding something to test Ella's DNA against. I can't take Tracy's word alone. There's too much at stake. Tracy told me she doesn't have any of Ella's belongings."

"How can I help?" Henry asked.

"I've had my people check for any medical or dental records, but we haven't been able to locate any, so I can't officially identify her as Ella. I'm wondering if someone from the church or the community might remember some personal details about Ella. Maybe if she was left-handed."

He knew it was a tall order, but he had to know. The woman waiting for him inside was most assuredly left-handed…just like Lena. But was Ella Weiss?

Henry's expression remained pensive. "I'll do what I can. My wife and I aren't from here originally, otherwise we could help you out. I'm not sure being left-handed is something anyone will remember, but there may be other avenues."

Some of the weight Kyle carried on his shoulders lifted. "I'd appreciate it. And thanks for the use of the cabin."

"No problem. I'll keep an eye on the local hospitals and medical facilities. If Peter Duncan shows his face, we'll have him."

As much as Kyle appreciated the watchful eye, he was pretty sure Duncan wouldn't dare seek medical help.

He clasped Henry's shoulder. "Thanks. To be on the safe side, the fewer calls made between us, the better."

Henry nodded. "I'll bring your car over later today. Molly can follow and drive me home. With that creep running loose and not knowing who all the players are, you'll need to have a way to escape should it come to that. Maybe I'll have something on the other matter by then." Henry got into his car and with one final wave drove away.

As Kyle listened to the vehicle leaving, he still didn't move. He couldn't get out of his head the memory of that last time he and Lena had spent together at their cabin. They'd gone there to celebrate their fifth wedding anniversary. It had been a special time. They'd talked about having children soon. Everything about it had been romantic and he'd been so much in love with her.

He swallowed back those heartbreaking thoughts and headed inside, where he found Ella mesmerized by the snowfall. She appeared worried about something.

"What is it?" he asked.

There were tears in her eyes. For a second he thought she might open up to him fully. Then just as quickly the vulnerability was gone and that stubborn defiance he'd grown to dislike returned. "Nothing. I guess I'm just tired."

He didn't challenge her. "After what happened back there, I'm feeling a little overwhelmed myself."

She seemed relieved that he didn't push her further.

"Do you want to rest for a bit?"

She shook her head. "Not really. But I am hungry." She smiled genuinely for the first time and it hit him that he couldn't remember seeing her smile before. It glued him in place. The way the left side of her mouth lifted just a little more in a lopsided grin. Lena had that same way of smiling, usually whenever she was teasing him.

Letting go of the similarities was hard, but he had to. They had a way of keeping him off balance, and he'd need a clear head to convince Ella to tell him what she hadn't shared so far.

"Henry said there's food. Let's see if there's something we can throw together for a meal."

She hesitated just a second. She seemed confused by his reaction to seeing her smile and yet he couldn't begin to explain. "That would be great," she said.

Kyle checked the fridge and found eggs and bacon and held them up. Her face lit up and she nodded.

"Oh, there's bread for toast," she said with a whimsical look.

He chucked and pulled out a frying pan. "Great." Before long, the savory aroma of frying bacon filled the cabin. It was nice to cook for more than one person. He'd gotten good at making quick meals for himself. After his baby sister, Emily, went away to college, more times than not he ended up pulling something together quickly.

"Breakfast is my favorite," she said casually and then stopped, her brows tangling in a frown.

Kyle tried to keep his feet under him at that revelation. "My wife used to love having breakfast for dinner, or lunch, for that matter. She could have eggs and bacon every day of the week…" He stopped when he got a good look at her expression. "What's wrong?"

She shook her head and forced a hint of a smile. "Nothing."

"My wife was with the CIA, as well," he continued, holding her gaze and watching as she processed the information.

"What happened to her?" she finally asked, her voice little more than a whisper. She looked as if everything hinged on his answer. He debated how much to give away. If he told her the details, would it be influencing her recollection?

He chose his words carefully. "She died," he said quietly.

Sympathy showed in her eyes. "I'm sorry. I can't imagine losing someone you love..." She stopped and then shook her head. But she clearly had lost someone, too. Her parents as well as her fiancé.

"Food's ready," he said, changing the subject and setting their plates on the table. "Do you want to say a prayer?"

She seemed uncertain and they sat in awkward silence. Another curious development.

Kyle bowed his head and prayed over the meal. "Father, thank You for safe passage today, for providing us food and shelter, and for always watching over us. Please be with Ella. Help her to regain her memories so that she can fully heal. Amen."

She didn't move; she simply stared out the window that reflected the snowy woods outside. Although her hands were at her sides, he could almost imagine them clenched in fists as she fought back tears.

"It's so beautiful here," she said at last. Her forehead scrunched into a thoughtful frown. "It reminds me of..." She shook her head. "I don't know what it reminds me of."

She was so lost. Although it had been a struggle from the beginning, he believed he'd gained just the tiniest bit of her trust. Kyle clasped her hand. Their gazes intertwined. His chest tightened. "It will come back to you, Ella. It's in there somewhere."

She squeezed his hand and then let go. "I hope you're right," she said without any real confidence. "I haven't been able to remember anything for years, so I'm not holding out hope. I sustained a bad injury when I was captured. Those first weeks in captivity, well, it's pretty much a blur, and I think I may have been drugged."

His jaw clenched when he thought about what Alhasan had done to her to ensure her cooperation. He couldn't imagine not being able to remember the things he took for granted every day—childhood, parents, falling in love, all being just out of your grasp.

"When I was in prison, all I thought about was surviving, and later on Joseph came." She paused briefly and studied the outside. "Then nothing else mattered. Just protecting him." Her face softened with love as she spoke of the boy. "He's so sweet and innocent. He didn't deserve what happened to his mother."

Kyle stared at her, uncertain he'd heard her correctly. "What happened to his mother?"

She didn't look at him. "She died. Alhasan killed her."

There had been another woman at the prison?

"Do you remember how long you were held there?" he asked and hoped she wouldn't shut him down completely.

She pushed her plate away. "I'm not sure. It felt like forever."

"I know it's hard thinking about that time," he said gently. "We don't have to talk about it if you don't want to."

She didn't answer. She got to her feet and carried her

plate over to the sink. "I'm alive, so it doesn't matter what happened to me back then. I have a second chance."

He came over to where she was. "It matters to me. I wish I could take away all your suffering," he said in earnest and as she stared up at him.

As he looked into Ella's eyes, there was no denying she felt the same pull he felt for her. She drew in a shaky breath. He so wanted to take her in his arms and kiss her. But was he simply transferring his feelings for Lena onto Ella?

He kissed her forehead instead. Disappointment etched itself on every inch of her face and she struggled to hide it.

"Kyle, we have to find Joseph before it's too late. If Alhasan's here then he's done what he said he would. He'll keep Joseph close to him. He knows how important he is to me. He'll be expecting me to do my part."

Lena had that same protective instinct about her. It helped her excel in her job, but had it also taken her life? If Lena had been there when Ella was captured, she'd have done whatever it took to protect her. Had it been the ultimate cause of her death?

He pushed Ella for more information. "What's your part? There's more that you haven't told me. I need to know everything."

Her gaze dropped to her hands. She twisted them nervously together. "I can't. He'll think I'm helping you." She backed away. "He told me if I did, he'd kill Joseph."

"What else does he want you to do?" He watched her shutting down in front of him. Her reaction was proof positive he'd hit it dead-on.

"I don't know what you're talking about," she murmured.

"You do. You said he wanted me dead, but there's

more that he wants you to do." When she didn't answer, he fought to get her to open up. "Ella, let me help you save the boy. You can't do it alone."

She turned and walked back into the living room and stared at the tranquility outside as if trying to find her own calm.

He understood why she didn't give her trust easily, but he had to find a way to tear down the wall of doubt she still held on to. "He's a liar. He'll tell you what you want to hear and then he'll break whatever promise he's made to you. Joseph still has a chance if you trust me."

Kyle stood behind her. His hands cupped her shoulders and drew her back against him. It thrilled him when she didn't pull away. Both their reflections were offered up in the window. He could read all her uncertainties as more of her story finally unfolded.

"He trained me for what I was to do," she said almost to herself. "He said as long as I did everything he told me, he'd keep Joseph alive." She stopped for the longest time. "But I can't do what he wants. I can't kill you or the rest of the Scorpions."

Kyle's couldn't hide his shock. "He wants you to take out the entire team? Why?"

She shook her head. "I don't know. He told me I was to find a way to get you to take me to your headquarters." She stared into his eyes reflected in the window. "And then kill your entire unit. He showed me photos of each of your team."

What could Alhasan possibly be after at their headquarters?

"There's something there that he can't find anywhere else," he concluded.

It took a second for what he said to click. "Yes, that makes sense."

"What's he after, Ella?"

She shook her head. "I don't know. He never said why he needed access, only that I had to do my part if I wanted Joseph alive."

He thought about Sam and his team. They'd been missing for way too long and now Liz and Michael were unaccounted for, as well. "I know this is hard, but I need you to try to think of anything else he might have said to you. Even if it seems insignificant."

Her dark eyes turned bleak. "Kyle, Alhasan is moving his entire operation to the US," she whispered. "And I think it's somehow connected to what he wants me to do."

In shock, he stared at her reflection for the longest time. Alhasan was moving his weapons smuggling operation to the United States? Kyle couldn't believe it. The probability of being caught moving weapons onto US soil was high. There could be only one reason why Alhasan would take that risk. He was planning something here.

Kyle decided it was time to tell her everything. "Ella, the people who went missing in Afghanistan the night you were rescued are still unaccounted for. Their time is running out. There may be others, as well. Please, I'm asking you to concentrate. Think. Anything you remember, no matter how small it seems, might help."

She shoved her fist against her head. "I'm trying. Don't you think I want to help?"

He struggled for calm and managed it. "I know you do," he said quietly. "Did he ever mention where he was setting up here?"

"I heard him speaking to someone once. He mentioned a place called Cedar Creek."

Kyle repeated the name in his head. He dug out his phone and typed it in. There were half a dozen Cedar Creeks around the country. One sent chills up his spine. It was a small logging town nestled on the southern Pennsylvania border. A little too close to the nation's capital for comfort.

If Alhasan was moving his business to the United States, then his new location might be closer than Kyle wanted to believe. Was that why he chose Ella? Because she was from Mountain Song and no one would suspect a missionary of being a terrorist? The insinuation was disturbing.

He met her gaze once more. There was more to come—he could see it in her troubled eyes. The only question was, which of them was it going to hurt the most?

"There was a man at the prison," she began slowly. Now that she'd put her trust in him, she knew she had to tell Kyle everything if she had any chance at saving Joseph. "He was an American."

"What did you say?" His stunned tone scared her. Did he believe her or would he think she was crazy?

She faced him knowing she had to look him in the eye. "There was an American man who visited the prison." She pulled much-needed air into her lungs and then told him what she suspected. "I think he's the real person in charge."

For the longest time, he didn't say a word, and her doubts rose.

"What you're saying is impossible, Ella." His tone was taut. "We know who's in charge. We've had him under surveillance for over a year now. I had an informant embedded in his operation. Alhasan never once led the informant to believe he answered to anyone. Alhasan is the one in charge."

Her thoughts were crystallizing more every second. She was positive of what she'd heard. She just had to find a way to convince Kyle. "You're wrong," she said passionately. "He made sure I never saw his face, but I heard him talking to Alhasan. He was an American and he's definitely the one calling the shots. Alhasan was fearful about angering him. And there's more. He had blond hair and he was tall…like Duncan."

His skepticism was difficult to take. "You're saying you think Duncan might be the real Fox? That's hard to believe."

She didn't understand. "Who is the Fox?"

He ran a hand across the back of his neck. "For the longest time, we didn't have a name for the terrorist who has been smuggling US military weapons out of Afghanistan. We believe he's stockpiling them for a future attack and who knows what else. We nicknamed him the Fox because he's very elusive. He's been operating in that region for years without being identified. He's responsible for countless attacks, including one that took the lives of several Scorpion team members. It's only been recently with the help of my asset that we were able to put a face as well as a name to the real Fox. And that name was Alhasan."

He shook his head. "Or so we thought. But if what you're saying is true, then what we believed we knew about the Fox and his plans are wrong. In other words, we're back to zero."

Suddenly everything she'd been so clear about came into doubt. Had she imagined the American's authoritative tone and Alhasan's desire to please him? What if she was wrong? She remembered the receipt she'd found at Duncan's home.

Ella pulled it out of her pocket and gave it to Kyle.

"What's this?" he asked as he stared into her eyes.

"With everything that's happened, I almost forgot. I found this at Duncan's house. It was stuck in a cookbook. I'm guessing he forgot he left it there."

Kyle stared at it and then her.

"I'm going to have my team take a closer look at Duncan's travels over the past ten years as well as his business. What else do you remember about the American? It's very important that you tell me everything about him."

She closed her eyes briefly and recalled the handful of times the American had been at the prison.

"He wasn't there all that much in the beginning, but when I heard him speak that first time, I knew he was an American." How had she been able to recognize the accent? She wasn't sure, but she'd known instinctively he was from the United States. "In the beginning the other woman was still there with me. But Alhasan hurt her badly." She drew in a breath. Let it go. "The American, he gave up on her. Said they'd never be able to break her. She was too strong."

"Who was she?" he asked in a strangled voice. Something was wrong.

"I'm not sure. She was nice to me. When I was first taken hostage, I was hurt badly." She touched the scar on her head. "She protected me. Stood between me and Alhasan. Helped me make it through those dark days." Ella shivered at the memory and looked at Kyle. All the color had left his face.

She was unaware of Kyle for the moment as she

thought back. "Alhasan called her…Lena. She helped me when I first arrived. I was in and out of consciousness. I couldn't remember anything about my past or who I was." She shook her head. "The surprising part was how alike we looked. It was almost like seeing my sister… Only that's not possible," she said almost to herself. "Lena was kind and sweet and she told me about God. I don't think I believed in Him before."

She struggled to hold on to another devastating memory. "Oh, Kyle. She was pregnant when I met her." Her gaze shot to his. The look of heartache written on his face made her wonder if she were seeing things that weren't there. Why had the mention of Lena brought him so much pain? The answer was in the dark edges of her mind but she was afraid to grasp onto it.

"Then one day, the American took her away. She never came back." Tears were close. She'd bottled up those dark memories. Now it was as if once they'd finally been freed, she couldn't hold them back.

"After a while, Alhasan brought me Joseph, told me he was Lena's child…" Another memory ripped at her heart, too fleeting to capture. It made her sad.

"I fought so hard to keep him safe. I named him Joseph because…" Was it a favorite name? The years of being drugged coupled with her head injury made it impossible to call up the memory. "I'm not sure why. Maybe Lena told me it was the name she wished for? Alhasan used my love for the child against me. He knew I'd do anything to protect Joseph, even if it meant losing my own life." She swallowed hard. "And now he's out there alone with Alhasan and I can't stand it. I let Joseph and Lena down." She brushed rough fingers across her tearstained cheeks. "Please, Kyle. I need your help. For Joseph. For Lena."

EIGHT

He stumbled away from her, the world around him spinning. The walls were closing in and he couldn't catch his breath. Ella had dropped a bombshell and he needed to be alone to process it.

He blindly headed for the door.

"Where are you going?" she implored. She didn't understand the heartbreaking pain tearing at his gut.

"Stay here. I'll only be a moment." He didn't wait for her answer.

The rejection he saw on her face was hard to take. But he couldn't bear to explain his actions right now.

He somehow managed to put one foot in front of the other until he reached the edge of the woods near the house. Kyle collapsed to his knees and buried his face in his hands.

The woman she called Lena had been pregnant. He couldn't believe it.

Despair brought tears to his eyes. Impossible, surely? It had to be a mistake. It wasn't his Lena, because there was no way she had been pregnant when she left on that mission. She would have told him. Even though he couldn't accept that the woman Ella spoke of might be his wife, the child she'd given birth to was still out there somewhere in the hands of the enemy.

Rage rose from the dark recess where he'd buried it years ago. He had no doubt that Alhasan was responsible for his wife's death. Ella was living proof of the cruelty the man was capable of.

He closed his eyes and prayed with all his heart that God would take away the anger and keep him clearheaded. He needed God to guide his hands. There was still a chance to save the boy. He had to stay resolute.

Kyle glanced around at the idyllic setting and a sense of peace settled around him. As he went over the things Ella had told him about the woman, too many things about her answers didn't add up for him to believe she was his wife.

When Lena went missing, she hadn't believed in God. When had that changed? Ella's disappearance had happened a year before Lena's. How could his wife have been at the compound before Ella?

Was Ella simply jumbling up memories or repeating lies Alhasan had told her? Was the whole accusation about the Fox being an American simply Alhasan planting doubts? Whatever the answer, it didn't change the truth in his mind. He'd buried his wife.

The noise of approaching vehicles drew his attention to the front of the house. He saw Henry's patrol car pulling up the drive, followed by the car Tracy had lent Kyle.

He went over to the patrol car.

"Thought you might need your transportation," Henry said through the open window.

Kyle smiled at the man's thoughtfulness. "Thanks. I appreciate it."

The driver of the car got out. It was a woman close to

Henry's age. Her gray hair cut short, she was dressed in jeans and a loose-fitting shirt.

She came over to the patrol car and Henry introduced her as his wife. "Agent Jennings, this is Molly."

The woman smiled up at Kyle. She appeared just as genuine as her husband.

"Nice to meet you, Agent Jennings," she told him and then handed Kyle the keys to the car.

"You, too," Kyle said and then added, "thanks for the use of the house."

"You're very welcome. Stay as long as you need." Molly turned back to her husband who nodded.

"We made sure no one followed us, but the less no-ticeable activity around the cabin the better." Once his wife was in the passenger seat, Henry put the vehicle in Reverse. "If you need anything at all, you call me. I can be here with backup in a matter of minutes."

Kyle nodded. "I will."

With Henry gone, he went back to the cabin.

Ella stood by the window watching for him. "Henry and his wife brought the car back in case we needed it," he said once he was inside. Still she didn't move.

He gathered a breath. Let it go. Prayed for calm. Found it. He needed to explain to her his emotional reaction earlier.

"My wife's name was Lena, as well," he said and she turned to face him, unable to hide her shock.

Slowly the story tumbled out as if he'd waited a long time to share it. "I told you she was CIA." He looked at her and was rewarded with the tiniest of nods. "Well, she was one of the best operatives I've ever worked with, and I loved her from the moment I met her…" His voice caught over the words and he stopped for a second. "I knew we were going to spend our lives together. I just didn't realize how short our time would be."

He slumped down onto the sofa, devoid of emotion. After a hesitant moment, Ella came and sat next to him.

"What happened to her?" she asked in a gentle tone.

He shook his head. That question had haunted him for years. "I wish I knew. The mission she was on was critical. A female operative with Lena's features and her fluency in the Dari language was necessary to go under-cover with an asset's family." His mouth twisted bitterly.

"Only you didn't want her to go," she guessed and he shot her a startled look. Had she read this from his expression?

"No," he said at last. "It didn't feel right to me. We'd vetted the family, so we knew they were friendlies. Still, I begged her not to take the mission. She went anyway."

Ella touched his arm gingerly. "I'm so sorry." He looked over at her and there were tears in her eyes.

"Back then, the Fox had just come onto our radar as a new player in arms smuggling. It was believed that he had roots in the village where the family Lena was stay-ing with lived. The family knew of him, which is why the idea of the Fox being an American doesn't ring true.

"Anyway, Lena was barely there a couple of weeks when the village where she was embedded got attacked. The family she'd been staying with was killed. Lena's body wasn't among the dead. We searched everywhere for her. Scoured the area. Called in every asset we could and interrogated dozens of people. Then about four months later, we found her body in the desert. She was burned beyond recognition." He swallowed at the hor-rific memory. "There were no dental records on file. Lena had never had so much as a cavity growing up, so as an adult she'd thought the dentist was a waste of time. I had to identify my wife through her wedding ring." It was the worst day of his life.

Kyle glanced down at the ring he still wore. He'd never once taken it off through the years, because something about his time with Lena felt unfinished. Maybe God had brought this woman into his life to give him the closure he so longed for.

Her voice shook when she spoke. "Do you have a picture of her?" He wondered if she was even aware she was crying. He was so unworthy of her sorrow. He should have done more to find his wife before she'd been killed.

He'd sensed even back then that something more was happening. He recalled how paralyzed he'd felt during Lena's final week at the village. Communication had been sketchy. He should have pulled her from the mission. He'd started to. Only he'd been too late. The village was raided. Lena was the one person left unaccounted for. Those frantic days before her body was discovered still haunted him.

Kyle dug out the photo he carried of Lena and himself at their cabin in Montana. He kept it with him always, because it was one of his favorite memories.

Ella took the photo from him and stared at it for the longest time.

"Is that the woman who was held with you?" he prompted.

She seemed incapable of speaking and his mind went crazy. She got to her feet and retreated to the windows once more.

"What is it?" He followed her. Something was wrong. This was not the reaction he'd expected. "Ella, tell me," he pressed. "Do you recognize the woman in the photo? Is that the Lena you knew at the prison?"

She didn't look at him. Kyle clasped her shoulders and gently turned her to face him. She appeared so distraught that all he wanted to do was comfort her. Take her in his arms and tell her it was going to be okay no matter what she remembered.

Ella clamped down on her bottom lip, pushed him away and fisted her hands. He'd seen this reaction many times. It was her coping mechanism. The frightening part was it mirrored his wife's to a T. Lena hated to cry. Hated showing the weakness.

"That's not her," she said with a hard tone. "That's not the woman I knew."

He couldn't determine if she was telling him the truth, but if so then who had been at the prison with Ella?

Before he could delve deeper, his cell phone rang. He recognized the number immediately. It was Tracy.

Tracy didn't wait for him to say hello. "Agent Jennings, I have to talk to you now," she said in a rush, her tone highly agitated.

"What's wrong?" he asked without taking his eyes off Ella.

"I can't say over the phone. Please, Agent Jennings, I have to speak to you in person immediately. It's urgent. It's about Ella," she whispered frantically.

Kyle's internal radar went crazy.

"I'm at the lake house. I came here to find you, but you were gone." She heaved an audible breath. "I'm in danger and so are you. He's going to kill me. Please hurry. Please, I need to tell you who Ella really is. Because I wasn't honest with you before. He forced me to lie."

His stomach dropped to his feet. Kyle glanced at his watch. "I'll be there in ten minutes."

Tracy's relief was clear. "Thank you. Thank you so much."

He disconnected the call and faced the questions in Ella's eyes.

"Something's wrong, isn't it?" she asked, her voice rough with the remnants of her tears.

"Yes. I have to go meet Tracy and I need you to come with me. I can't leave you here alone, Ella. It's not safe."

Kyle prayed he wasn't making a huge mistake by taking her with him. He had to keep her close to protect her. His emotions were still raw from the roller-coaster ride he'd been on since the desert.

He grabbed the extra Glock and burner phone from where she'd placed them on the kitchen counter.

"I need you to wait in the car. I don't know what I'll find once I get there. Tracy said someone wanted her dead." He could see the terror those words brought as Ella followed him out to the car.

Kyle covered the distance between the cabin and the lake house in record time. His trained instinct told him not to go directly to the house. Instead, he pulled the car into a wooded area off to the side of the main highway, still some distance from the house.

"It's safer here and we're out of sight. I can get there by going through those woods there." He pointed to the forest. "I should end up at the side of the house. No one watching it will know I'm coming and you should be sheltered here."

Kyle pulled out his Glock and checked the clip. It was full. He put a spare clip in his pocket.

"Let me come with you," she pleaded. "I can back you up should something turn sideways."

His hand rested on the door as he tried to shut out the way she worded things as if… "It's too risky. It could be a setup."

"Kyle…" Her voice cracked. "Haven't I proven by now that I know what I'm doing?"

He struggled to keep his equilibrium. That was word for word something Lena would say. He had to let go of that hope once and for all.

He sucked in a breath. "We can't chance a repeat of what happened at Duncan's place. We have no idea who or what we're up against anymore. Wait here. Lock the doors and stay low." He pointed to the Glock next to her on the seat. "Keep that and the phone close. If anything happens, call me right away."

He hated to leave her alone, but Tracy's tone was warning enough to ensure what she had to tell him was going to be big.

"If I don't get in touch with you in five minutes, call Henry."

They stared at each other for the longest time. She looked at him with those expressive eyes that tugged at his heart. He didn't want to make the same mistake he'd made all those years ago.

He had no idea what he faced inside. His last moments with Lena stood out in his head and he didn't want to let this moment pass without expressing what was in his heart. He leaned close and captured her lips. A tiny sob escaped and then she framed his face with her hands and kissed him back. Her touch felt like Lena's. All heart-breaking.

He reluctantly ended the kiss. Clearing away the frog

from his throat wasn't easy. "It'll be okay. Just remember what I said. If I don't call you back soon, get out of here and find help."

She nodded and he slowly let her go. With one final searching look, he got out of the car and headed for the woods.

As he moved through the thicket, his thoughts were all for the woman he'd left behind. There had been something in the way she looked at the photo. He was almost positive she had recognized it.

Stop it!

When he reached the edge of the property, he stopped. A small car was parked in the drive. Nothing appeared out of order. Still, Tracy's fear had been obvious and the nervous knot in the pit of his stomach warned him not to let his guard down.

Kyle slowly eased from his cover and advanced toward the house with weapon in hand. The front door stood open, his breathing quickening with adrenaline. A round of shots came from inside.

He grabbed his phone and called Henry. "I need you here at the lake house right away. I have shots fired. Bring EMT." Kyle rushed inside without waiting for Henry's response. More shots followed. Then a woman screamed.

"Tracy, where are you?" he called out while searching for the shooter.

"In the kitchen. I think he's gone," she croaked in a barely audible voice.

He carefully scanned the visible rooms. No one was there. Where had the shooter gone? He tucked the Glock behind his back and rushed to Tracy's side. She'd been shot in the chest and was seriously injured. He took off his jacket and balled it up against her wound to slow the blood flow.

"Hang on, I've called for help," he said to keep her calm. She didn't listen. She was looking just beyond him.

She managed to lift her finger at something over his shoulder.

Kyle jerked around in time to see a man dressed in dark clothing lunge for him. He jumped to his feet and successfully evaded a direct hit. He didn't recognize the man, but the anger that flashed on the man's face bordered on maniacal.

The man had a gun aimed at Kyle's head. "You shouldn't have come here. You should have gone where you were supposed to," he snarled.

Kyle kicked the kitchen table sideways and ducked as the man opened fire. Several shots barely missed him.

"You can't hide, Agent Jennings. You're going to die. The same way your wife did. I enjoyed ending her life." Kyle froze at the man's confession to killing his Lena. "Ending yours will be my pleasure, as well."

A storm of anger propelled Kyle to his feet. He charged the man, the action taking him by surprise. The man aimed the weapon straight at him. Kyle had only seconds to reach him before it discharged. There was no way he'd make it in time. A thousand regrets flew through his head. Then he heard it. *Click, click, click.* The weapon was empty.

The man tossed the useless gun aside and pulled out an equally deadly knife.

He came after Kyle full charge. With all his strength, Kyle shoved him off, but he just kept coming back, like a raging animal intent on taking down his prey.

Kyle drew his weapon. His first instinct was to shoot

to kill, but this man had confessed to taking Lena's life. He wanted him alive, because he needed to know more.

The second he was in striking distance, Kyle smashed the butt of the Glock against his head. The man dropped to the floor, out cold.

Kyle quickly secured the assailant's hands. Was he here alone? Somehow he doubted it. If there were more men roaming the countryside, Ella could be in danger. He tried the phone. There was no signal. He tried it again. Nothing. Impossible. He'd just called…unless someone had deliberately blocked the call. His first instinct was to rush back to Ella's side and make sure she was safe, but he couldn't leave Tracy. She was terrified.

"It's going to be okay," he told her as calmly as he could while examining Tracy's wound. It was much worse than he thought. The bullet had struck close to her heart.

Nearby, sirens blared. "Hang on. The ambulance is almost here."

She shook her head. "I'm not going to make it and I can't die knowing I've lied to you. I have to tell you the truth about Ella Weiss."

Ella had watched him disappear. He'd been gone for a while, and yet still she couldn't move. Her head was bursting with confusing memories. Had been ever since Kyle showed her the photo of his wife. She'd told him that wasn't the woman held prisoner with her, but that wasn't the complete truth. It wasn't the woman she knew as Lena. It was…

She still clutched the crumpled photo in her hand.

The cabin in the mountain she'd remembered from before was there in the background. She and Kyle had been there many times during their marriage. The last time was before she left for that final mission. It had been a picture-perfect vacation. Snowing every day. They'd made a fire...

No...that's not your life. It can't be. You're Ella.

She fisted her hand against her forehead. There was more, much more to the story. Something dark was hidden away inside her head and now it was ready to take life and there was nothing she could do to stop it.

"No." Another broken sob escaped. She'd struggled to hold them back since he'd showed her the photo.

She touched her stomach. That was the worst part. She'd been pregnant when she left on that final mission, and she hadn't told him. She and Kyle had argued. He didn't want her to go. He'd told her he had a bad feeling about it. Begged her to let someone else do the job for once, but she couldn't. The arrangements were all made. The family trusted her. It was too late to substitute another agent. She'd made a fateful mistake.

She closed her eyes. Her baby. She'd given birth. Alhasan had taken delight in telling her the baby was a girl and that the child was stillborn. Her grief pleased him. She'd been comatose with despair for weeks afterward.

Would Kyle blame her for their child's death? After all, she'd insisted on going on that mission. If she'd just listened to her husband, their child would still be alive. They'd be happy. It was her fault that their daughter died.

The grief she'd hidden away so long sliced through her heart. She buried her head in her hands and gave in to the pain.

Outside, the noise of a car on the road nearby captured her attention. Someone was coming. Kyle had told her to stay here, but if it was the enemy, she would be an easy target.

She got out of the car and rushed to the woods. The noise of the vehicle grew closer. She peered through the trees as the car that had attacked them at the church stopped on the side of the road. This wasn't just someone traveling by. The people in the car were deliberately looking for them. *Her*. She spotted the driver and her blood ran cold. Alhasan. There was another man with him. No doubt others, as well.

They didn't make a move to get out. Were they waiting for backup before they attacked? How did they find her?

Everything will work out the way it's supposed to in time. If you do your part...

She recalled what Tracy had said to her outside the church and her fear for Kyle doubled. Was Tracy working for Alhasan and had she made the call to draw him out so that these men could kill him?

She grabbed the phone. The call didn't go through. She tried again with the same results. There was no signal.

She glanced at the car. Alhasan got out along with three more men. "You might as well give up, Ella. No one's coming to help you." Fear shot through her. How did he know she was there? And more important, where was Joseph? Wouldn't he have brought the child along to use as leverage to get her to do his bidding?

She ducked behind the tree coverage. If the calls were being blocked, did Alhasan have that much power, or was Henry working with him?

"He's not going to help you. He'll be dead by now," Alhasan sneered and Ella's heart fell to her feet.

No. Please keep him safe.

She wouldn't stand a chance if she stayed here. If she

could reach one of the houses close by, perhaps someone would be home. She could call for help.

From where she stood, she could see the back of a neighboring house about a quarter of a mile to the left. If she reached it, she might have a chance. Once they stormed the woods, they'd search every inch. It would buy her some precious time.

She hurried through the dense undergrowth, praying every step of the way that Alhasan didn't have men circling behind. The brisk air robbed her of her breath.

"He needs her alive for now," Alhasan shouted to his men. "She knows things. Find her. She can't be far."

Did this have something to do with Alhasan wanting access to the Scorpions' headquarters? What did they need there that was so important?

Another car crunched on the gravel on the edge of the road before coming to a stop. Alhasan's backup.

Car doors slammed. Multiple footsteps followed. She had to hurry.

She reached the thickest part of the woods and was forced to slow down. She'd lost sight of the house. She had no idea if she was still heading in the right direction. She prayed for clarification and hoped she'd receive it as she kept heading left. Five minutes had passed. Behind her she could still hear Alhasan's rantings.

"All right, we'll do this the hard way, but I'll make you pay, Ella. You'll pay dearly." Silence followed then multiple footsteps fanning quickly out through the woods.

Fear propelled her on. Once the men figured the direction she'd gone in the snow, they'd find her easily enough.

She had to keep moving. She ran as fast as she could, tripping over downed branches along the way.

"This way. I see her up ahead," one of the men yelled to the group. She gasped for breath. She could see the clearing up ahead. Almost there. She raced as fast as her body would allow and hit the clearing. The house.

She ran up the steps and pounded on the door. "Please help me. Someone's trying to kill me." She could hear footsteps at the back of the house. Someone was coming.

Thank You, God.

She peeked behind her. The men chasing her were now at the clearing. They'd see her at the front of the house. She headed for the back when she all but slammed into someone.

Relief weakened her legs.

"Thank you—" Her words died away when she saw who it was. Her worst nightmare. Duncan.

He grabbed her and yanked her close. "You're so predictable. I knew you would come here, just as I knew you wouldn't do what you were supposed to do."

The men following reached her. Alhasan was with them. Joseph was nowhere in sight. Her heart plummeted. Where was the boy?

"Clear out of here in case he returns. You know where to rendezvous." Alhasan barked the order to his men then glared at her. "She's coming with me."

Duncan shoved her that way. Alhasan grabbed her hair and hauled her to the car. She knew if he took her away, her chances of surviving were slim. She had to think quickly. Find a way to escape.

He shoved her inside then got in beside her. She scrambled for the passenger door, but he grabbed her by her hair again.

"I don't think so," he said as hauled her back against him.

She fought him with everything she had. All she could think about was Joseph.

"Where is he?" she screamed at him. "What have you done to Joseph?"

Alhasan laughed in her face. "What do you think?" he mocked.

"No," she whimpered as the reality of what he said registered. Tears streamed down her face. He'd killed Joseph. Taken that innocent life.

Fury rose from deep inside and with all her strength she jerked free and clawed at his face. Blood sprang from the imprint of her nails. She wanted him to pay for what he'd done.

He recoiled in pain. He touched the blood, staring at it and then at her in surprise. Before she could get away he slapped her so hard that her head spun in the opposite direction.

"You foolish woman. I should have known you wouldn't follow through with the plan. You're too loyal to the cause…and him. That's why we had to keep track of you. You failed us. So now, you and I have some unfinished business. Once *he's* done with you, it will be my pleasure to end your life like I did the boy's."

NINE

The sirens were right outside. Tracy was barely hanging on.

"You have to forgive me," she begged and clasped his hand tightly. "Please...you have to."

He tried to reassure her. "It's going to be okay. Don't try to talk."

She ignored him and motioned for him to come closer. "He made me do it," she rasped. There were tears streaming down her face. "I'm so sorry. I should have known it wasn't real."

"Who, Tracy? Who are you talking about?" he whispered urgently.

She struggled to draw air in, her voice barely there. "He told me he loved me. He said he was with the CIA and that I was doing my country a huge service by following his command. I'd be helping him bring down a terrorist." She gathered her strength. As much as he needed her to rest, he had to hear her story.

"He wanted me to identify a woman as Ella Weiss and keep an eye on her," she rasped. "He said that she was part of a terrorist cell that would be operating here in the US. That's why I couldn't tell you anything before."

Kyle took out the photo of Alhasan. "Is this the man?" Tracy glanced at the photo and shook her head.

"No, the man I fell in love with is called Jonathan. He has blond hair and blue eyes."

Who was this Jonathan and how was he connected to the Fox? Was it possible Ella might be right and Duncan was the man they'd been hunting all along?

Kyle found the photo Jase sent him of Duncan and showed it to her.

"That's not him." Could Tracy be wrong? The man could have changed his appearance to throw them off.

Tracy gathered her waning strength. "I realized when I saw how he'd hurt her that she was no terrorist. He was just using me. I tried to get out. That's when he sent someone to kill me and you walked in on the attack."

In his mind, Tracy's story just confirmed what Ella said about the Fox not being Alhasan. The only question that remained was if she wasn't Ella, then…

Outside, doors slammed. EMTs raced into the house followed by Henry and some of his men.

Kyle leaned over and whispered his thanks to Tracy. "Hang on, Tracy. Don't you dare give up." She managed a weak nod and he let the professionals take over.

He went over to Henry and told him everything.

"I have to go. Ella's out there alone. She could be in danger." He headed for the door when Henry stopped him.

"Take some of my men with you."

Kyle didn't answer. He grabbed the phone and tried to call the burner once more. The call failed. His uncertainties grew.

"I parked on the main road," he told one of the deputies who came with him. "Can you give me a lift to the vehicle?"

"Absolutely." One of the deputies got behind the wheel and another climbed into the back while Kyle hopped in the passenger seat.

"It's just up here," Kyle told him. Once their vehicle stopped, he got out and hurried to the car. The second he was close, he noticed it was empty. Ella wasn't there.

"Ella," he called out.

His only answer was tires squealing close by.

"She's been taken," Kyle yelled to the two deputies before he jumped into the car and drove as fast as he could out of the wooded area. The deputies followed at a high speed.

Up ahead, he spotted the car from the church. He could see two people inside. As he drew close, he was positive the driver was Alhasan. And Ella was with him.

Alhasan had Ella.

Kyle floored the gas until he was inches from the bumper.

Alhasan must have been watching in the rearview mirror. When he spotted Kyle, he rolled the window down and opened fire. Kyle swerved to keep from a direct hit. The patrol car behind him hit its emergency lights.

He couldn't let Alhasan escape again. If he did, Ella would be dead. Kyle made the decision to take extreme measures. He rammed the car hard and sent it flying off the road. It crashed into the ditch nose first. Smoke billowed from the hood.

Kyle slammed on the brakes and jumped from the vehicle as Alhasan stumbled out, firing.

The patrol car stopped behind them. The two officers

exited with weapons drawn and ducked behind their vehicle.

Realizing he was outnumbered, Alhasan raced for the nearby woods.

"Go after him," Kyle called to the officers and they immediately pursued. But Kyle's only thoughts were for Ella's safety. He hurried to her side.

"Are you hurt?" he asked in a fear-threaded voice. He didn't wait for her answer. He did a quick check of her limbs. Nothing was broken and Kyle whispered his prayerful thanks under his breath. She had a few scrapes, yet for the most part, she was physically unscathed but clearly terrified.

She went into his arms and clung to him and he held her tight. God had protected her and he was so grateful.

She withdrew a shuddering breath and pulled away. "I'm okay," she reassured him. "I'm okay. I was so scared. I tried to get away but they found me."

He cupped her face. All his fear and worry over what might have happened was reflected in his voice. "I'm so sorry I wasn't there to protect you, Lena, but I promise I won't let anything happen to you again."

Something in her eyes tore at his gut.

"What is it?" he asked.

She shook her head and he lifted her into his arms and carried her to the car.

Kyle noticed the two officers emerging from the woods without Alhasan. Had the man escaped? They motioned to him. He didn't want to leave her alone but he needed to find out what had happened. He touched her cheek and looked deep into her eyes. "I'll be right back, okay?"

He cracked the door open and started out when she grabbed his arm. "Kyle…"

Something troubled her, but again she kept it to herself. Her expression grew suddenly distant. "Be careful," she said instead of what he was certain she'd wanted to say.

He'd called her *Lena*. Tears filled her eyes. He hadn't even realized the slipup. Did he believe she was Lena, too? Her head spun with the returned memories. If she could turn back time, she'd change so many things. But that was an impossible wish, and she didn't know how to tell him about the baby.

She watched as Kyle spoke briefly with the officers then headed back to the car. She was struck again by how handsome, strong and self-assured he was. A true man of valor. Her husband. Did she dare tell him she knew that truth? She steeled herself to face him again.

He started the vehicle and turned to her. "There's no sign of him. I can't believe he got away. They'll keep searching. Henry has other men on the way to help out. We can't go back to the cabin." His gaze narrowed as he watched her. "What's troubling you?" he asked gently.

As she met his gaze, all the love she felt for him surfaced and she cupped his face and drew him near. She kissed his lips and felt him freeze for a second, then kiss her back like only Kyle could. His lips so familiar, so welcoming, that she wanted to keep right on kissing him and never have to face the reality of her decisions. But it was not to be.

She pulled away. "I'm sorry…" She couldn't look at him. Until she'd kissed him now—with the realization that she might be Lena—she hadn't been completely sure. Now there was no doubt. This was her husband. For the first time in years the ice surrounding her heart had melted away and she was finally free to feel.

After a second, he took her hand and squeezed it. "It's okay. We both got a little carried away." The gentle teasing in his tone forced her to look at him. She remembered all those times in the past when he'd looked that same way. Kyle could always make her wonder if he was serious or joking.

She smiled back. "Yes, you're right." She cleared her throat. "What do we do now?"

His gaze never wavered. "I know you don't want me to, but it's time to call in the Scorpions. It's not safe for either of us to be here any longer. Once the team arrives, we can figure the rest of it out," he said, and she realized he hadn't understood what she meant. She wondered where *they* went from here, but then, he didn't know her memory had returned.

"I'm thinking we go back to the church." Before she could react he said, "Hear me out first." And she slowly nodded.

"I know it's a gutsy move, but after what happened there before, they won't be expecting us to return. We just need to stay out of sight until the team arrives." When she didn't answer, he said, "I'll call the pastor once we've stashed this car. They'll be looking for it."

"That sounds like a good plan," she managed.

He gave her another quizzical look he put the car in Drive.

Since seeing the photo she had tucked in her pocket, it was as if the dam holding her memories captive had broken. Her life with Kyle was rushing out jumbled and confused. She so desperately needed to be alone to figure it all out. She closed her eyes. The baby. Their little girl. She could almost picture her… Her eyes flew open. No, that couldn't be. Alhasan had taken that opportunity away. Hate rose inside her. She'd buried it, as well. She had so much of it in her heart. She couldn't let it control her.

Please take it away.

"I think we should leave the car in town and walk to the church," Kyle said and she rousted herself from those dreadful memories. He glanced her way. "Are you up to it? You've been through a lot lately."

She quickly reassured him. "I'll be fine."

He pulled into the parking lot of a restaurant and parked as far out of the passing traffic's line of sight as possible.

When she reached for the door, he stopped her. "Did something else happen at the cabin?"

She met his eyes. Would she find the forgiveness she needed? She swallowed back a sob. "No, it's just been a very long day."

She could see he didn't believe her fully.

Kyle got out of the car and came round to her side as she did the same.

"What did Tracy need to talk to you about?" she asked, mostly because she so desperately needed to shut out the darkness.

His hesitation captured her full attention. They started walking without an answer.

"Kyle?" Her heart pumped into overdrive.

"Not much," he said at last. "Someone shot her. When I arrived, I was attacked. She's on her way to the hospital. It doesn't look good. Henry took the shooter into custody. Once the rest of the team is here, we'll see what he knows."

He paused for a second and she knew she'd been right about Tracy being involved with Alhasan.

"Tracy pretty much confirmed what you said about the real person in charge not being Alhasan. She was fooled by someone fitting Duncan's description, only it wasn't him."

"Was she sure?" she asked in amazement. But then again, she'd heard Duncan speak. His voice wasn't the same as the American's. He nodded. "Oh, yes. She said the man who recruited her used her feelings for him to get her to do his bidding. She only knew him as Jonathan. I showed her Duncan's photo, it wasn't him. She said the man she knows has blue eyes."

She couldn't wrap her mind around what he told her. "Why would he want Tracy to work for him… It's because of me."

"Yes," he confirmed. "In fact, she claims he told her to identify you as Ella Weiss even though she believes that's not who you are. The man told her you were a terrorist. That's how he got her to cooperate."

That had been the one thing that didn't add up. How had Tracy known her? Now she realized the truth. Tracy was right. She wasn't Ella at all. She was Lena. She was Kyle's wife. Her heart had been screaming that from the beginning, but she just hadn't remembered.

"I'm not Ella," she said to herself.

He continued to watch her with an unreadable expression, one she'd seen many times recently. "No, you're not," he said quietly.

The final obstacle holding her back was gone. She wasn't the person she'd believed herself to be.

Right there in the middle of the sidewalk, she lost it.

Tears streamed from her eyes. Of course she wasn't Ella. Ella had been the one to die, not her. *She* was still alive.

"Hey, we'll figure it out." Kyle tugged her into the shelter of his arms and moved close to the storefront and away from prying eyes.

He didn't understand. How did she tell him the ugly secrets of her heart? She shook her head miserably.

"I promise you we'll do everything we can to find out who you really are." He was trying so hard, but he didn't sound convinced.

She pushed away. That wasn't the problem. She knew that part of the puzzle. The only question was would he forgive her.

"I know who I am, Kyle. I've known for a while."

TEN

He couldn't believe he'd heard her correctly. "What do you mean, you know who you are?" It didn't compute. If she knew she wasn't Ella, why hadn't she told him? His heart thudded in his chest. Had he been wrong about her all along? Was she working for Alhasan?

"How do you know?"

With tears shimmering in her eyes, she pulled something from her pocket and handed it to him. Like a robot, he tore his gaze from hers and glanced down. It was the photo he'd shown her of him and Lena. She'd held on to it.

She could barely speak, but she pushed on. "At first, well, I didn't understand. Nothing made sense. It went against everything I was told."

"Ella, please..." He closed his eyes and held on to his heart by a thread. "Please just tell me."

She wiped her palm over her tears. "This is hard. I still can't believe it. But you see, nothing I was told about my past made sense. I didn't feel it here." She pointed to her heart. "Then you showed me this and it just all fell into place. I know this will sound crazy. It does to me, too, but I recognize the cabin in that photo. I remember the times we spent there together. Our honeymoon. It was so special…" She stopped, almost as if she was afraid to go on.

Kyle felt as if someone had taken his carefully ordered world and thrown it to the wind.

"And your wedding ring. The second I saw it I remembered it. And then when I kissed you, I knew." She pulled in a breath. "This is me, Kyle." She pointed to the photo. "The woman in that photo is me. I'm Lena. I'm your wife."

His face crumpled and everything suddenly made sense for him, as well. He hadn't let himself have hope until now. His heart swelled and he gathered her closer. He'd known. From the moment he met her in the desert—even though he'd refused to accept it—he knew this was his Lena. It was as if his very heart had connected to hers the second he found her.

"Oh, Lena. Oh, my Lena." His voice tightened with tears but he didn't care. This was his wife. He'd thought she was lost to him forever and now she'd come home to him.

"I can't believe it. I can't believe it. I'm so happy to have you back." He held her like a lifeline. He had to keep telling himself he wasn't dreaming. This was real. She was real. God had given him back his wife.

She pushed at his chest. "You felt it, too?" she asked in amazement and touched his face, as if she still couldn't believe she'd found him again.

"From the beginning. I couldn't understand it, either, and it went against everything I was told about what happened, but I knew you were my wife."

He took her hand and kissed her palm. She flinched and tried to pull away, but he wouldn't let her. "No, babe, no. You are so beautiful to me and I am happy to have you back. So very happy," he said in a tone broken by emotion as he cupped her face and kissed her with all his heart. Nothing else mattered but her. His wife.

He became aware of several curious people passing by. As much as he wanted to keep on kissing her, he knew the enemy could be any of those people around them.

"We should probably get to the church and out of sight as soon as we can," he said in a breathless tone.

"Yes," she said and smiled up at him.

He took her hand and held it tight as they headed for the church. She caught him checking behind them several times.

"Is someone back there?" When she would have followed his line of sight, he stopped her.

"I don't think so, I'm just being cautious." He smiled to try to reassure her and she returned his smile.

"Let's stop in here for a second," he told her and they ducked into a coffeehouse. He drew her closer. "I just want to make sure we weren't followed. The sooner I get you out of this area and safely to Scorpion headquarters, the better."

She snuggled close. "I love you, Kyle. I love you so much."

He stared at her in wonder. He never thought he'd hear those words from her again and it scared him to death. He had so much to lose. He'd found her again. What if he couldn't keep her safe?

"I love you, too, babe. I love you, too."

He watched the passing foot traffic until he was sure no one was particularly interested in them. "I need to call Jase. Have him get the team airborne right away."

Tears filled her eyes. "Jase." She said the name in surprise. "I almost forgot about my old partner. How is he?"

"He's good. He's married and he and his wife have a child on the way."

"Jase is married?" Her surprise was easy to read. He chuckled. He certainly understood her confusion. The Jase she'd known was all work. He'd lived, breathed and slept the job. She didn't know what he'd been through. His former girlfriend Abby's betrayal. The threat against him and Reyna.

He filled her in on what had happened in the years she'd been gone.

"Poor Jase. To be betrayed by someone he loved like that." There was something in her tone he couldn't define. It alarmed him. Was it just because of Jase's hurt?

"Yes. But he's happy now and he's going to be so tickled to see you again. We all thought we'd lost you for good."

She managed a smile and he took out his phone and dialed. Even after he'd told Jase everything that had happened, he could tell his friend was having trouble processing the truth.

"Lena's alive? That's…amazing. Unbelievable." Jase stopped for a second and then asked, "How's she holding up to the news?"

He glanced down at his wife. His wife! He still couldn't get used to saying those words.

He turned slightly away and pretended to study the crowd around them. "She's struggling. I've never seen Lena so uncertain before." He swallowed the lump in his throat. "She has a long road ahead of her to adjust to the new way of life. We both do."

"But she's alive. That's huge. We'll be praying for you both. The best thing we can do for her is to get her someplace where she can truly feel safe to heal."

Kyle blew out a breath. "I couldn't agree more. Every minute she's here her life is in danger."

"And yours, as well... Hang on a second," Jase told him. Kyle could hear his friend talking to someone. "That was Aaron. I'm afraid I have bad news. We have a vicious storm moving through. We're grounded until it passes. Let's hope it won't be too long."

Aaron Foster was the team's pilot and one of the best military trainers Kyle had ever worked with. Jase paused for a second longer and Kyle could tell there was more bad news to follow.

"What is it?" he asked.

Jase sighed. "With everything that's happened, I hate to pile this on you, but I spoke to Dalton earlier. He couldn't reach you. They've located Liz and Michael's phones in the desert not too far from where the compound went up. We have no idea where they are, Kyle, or what happened to them, for that matter."

It was his worst nightmare—having his agents go missing. First Sam and his team and now Liz and Michael. Of all people, Liz knew how dangerous the Fox was. She wouldn't deliberately put her life and her partner's in danger.

"I'm hoping we'll have some answers soon. Hang in there, brother. I'll let you know the minute we're in the air."

Kyle disconnected the call and put his phone away. "He can be here in five hours if the storm that's hitting the area passes soon."

There was a fear in her eyes that the old Lena wouldn't have comprehended. They both had so much more to lose. Their fragile future.

Kyle headed for the door when a man with a knit cap

pulled low on his head stepped close and into his personal space. Something hard was shoved against his side. Right away he knew it was a gun.

"Got ya," the man sneered. Kyle didn't recognize him, but he knew instinctively that it was one of the Fox's goons.

"Don't try anything stupid, Jennings. You and the wife here need to play nice and come with us. My men are right outside. You can still be of use to us. Get us into your headquarters. We don't need her. I won't think twice about killing her and anyone else who gets in our way."

Another man stepped beside Lena, took hold of her arm and pulled her free of Kyle. His fear for her safety skyrocketed.

He struggled to portray calm. "Leave her alone. I'll do what you want, but leave her. You said yourself you don't need her."

The man laughed. "You think I don't know what you're trying? She'll call the cops as soon as we're out of sight." He motioned to his guy, who dragged Lena out of Kyle's reach.

Kyle had to come up with a plan and quickly. He'd shoved the cell phone back in his pocket. If he could just redial Jase's number...

He punched the call button and tried not to bring attention to himself while praying he'd done everything correctly. Once he hit what he believed was the speaker button, he hoped Jase had picked up and would call Henry for help.

"We'll go with you. There's no need to hurt anyone."

The man with the cap glared at him suspiciously for the longest time.

Please don't let him figure out what I'm doing.

"Don't tell me what to do, Jennings. You and your wife have caused enough trouble. He's not happy with the way things are going. You're messing with our schedule. We've had to chase after you two when we should be—" He stopped as if realizing he'd said too much.

Lena's gaze shot to Kyle. He couldn't imagine what was going through her mind. She had to be terrified of being captured again. He prayed with all his heart that the call went through and backup was on the way.

"Let's go. Stop stalling," the man barked and yanked at his arm and several patrons glanced their way curiously, forcing the man to stop. He smiled. "Come on, buddy, we're going to be late for our meeting."

With the second man gripping Lena's arm, Kyle was forced out the door first.

Kyle searched the area but didn't see a single welcome sight.

"This way," the man ordered and pointed toward a black sedan parked a few cars away. They'd changed vehicles. No one would be looking for this one.

As they approached the car, Kyle noticed there were two additional men inside. They wouldn't stand a chance once they were in the vehicle. They'd be powerless. It was now or never.

Lena wasn't close enough to touch, but he could see she was watching him carefully, waiting for a sign. He tapped his arm twice and saw her nod.

Kyle caught the man off guard, jerked free and quickly drew his weapon. He grabbed the man's arm and forced it behind his back. Before Lena's captor could respond, she slugged him hard in the midsection. He doubled over in pain, gasping for air. She immediately grabbed his weapon and aimed it at his head.

"Don't try anything foolish," she told him.

The remaining two men shot from the vehicle with their weapons aimed at Kyle and Lena.

Kyle pushed the Glock against the man's temple. "If you want him to live, stay where you are."

Both men stopped dead in their tracks.

"Shoot them," the man in Kyle's grasp yelled. The men stared at each other, unsure what to do. Several people standing nearby screamed and dove for cover. Hopefully, one of them would call 911.

"I wouldn't if I were you," Kyle warned. "You'll be dead before you can get a single shot off."

The men didn't seem nearly as loyal to the cause.

"Kill them or I'll kill you," the man with the cap continued ranting.

"This is nuts. I'm not dying for you or him," one of the men said. He dropped his weapon. The second man did the same.

"Do you know what you've done?" the angry man admonished, his irritation boiling in his tone. "We'll all be dead. Traitors aren't allowed. You've seen what he's capable of. You know what he'll do to us."

One thing became clear. None of these men were the one in charge. They were terrified of being labeled traitors and subsequently losing their lives.

The man with the cap gave it one final try. "Fight, you fools. You have to fight them. We can still salvage this."

"Shut up," Kyle ordered. "Both of you—get your hands in the air." The two men rushed to do as he commanded.

Kyle picked up sirens coming their way. Jase had gotten the message. Seconds later, the place was crawling with cops. Henry was one of them. The chief took a second to assess the scene before ordering his officers to restrain all the men. Two deputies holstered their weapons and rushed forward.

Kyle didn't dare let go of the man in his grasp. He'd proven he had nothing to lose.

"I got him, Agent Jennings," Henry said and took the man from him. Kyle realized his hands were shaking.

After another deputy handcuffed Lena's prisoner, she ran to Kyle's side and he held her close. They'd come so close to being captured by the Fox's men. They might not get away the next time.

"If you two were cats, I'd say you've used up about eight of your nine lives by now," Henry told them as he handed off his prisoner. "And you're filling up my jail pretty quick."

Kyle managed a smile. "Hopefully you have room for a few more."

"I think we can accommodate." Henry motioned toward the men being shuffled off into patrol cars. "Looks like our elusive Peter Duncan and Alhasan are still at large."

That was one of the most disturbing parts. "Yes, they could be anywhere. Their men are well trained and brazen. That one shoved a gun in my side and threatened to take out anyone who got in their way, including Lena."

Henry shook his head in disbelief. "They are ruthless. Maybe one of these guys will talk and we can find out where the others are holed up."

Kyle wished he could believe it was that easy. But the Fox had a hold on his people. They were loyal to him out of fear for their lives.

What Kyle had said earlier finally registered and Henry asked, "Wait, did you call her Lena… I thought your name was Ella Weiss?" Clearly confused, he glanced at Lena, who smiled.

"No, I'm Lena Jennings. I'm Kyle's wife. It's a long story," she added sympathetically when Henry's frown deepened.

"When this is over, you'll have to fill me in. Sounds like a crazy one." Henry shook his head and watched as his deputies drove the prisoners away. "Probably not safe for you to be out here in the open like this with those other ones still running around. What can I do to help?" Henry asked.

Kyle was overwhelmed by the man's generosity. "I'm not sure. I'd planned on texting the pastor to see if we can take sanctuary at the church for a while, but after what happened now, well…"

Henry was quick to assure him. "You can trust James. He's a good man and I'm thinking Alhasan won't be expecting you to return to the church."

With no other option at the moment, Kyle hoped the chief's opinion proved true. "I'll let him know we're coming. The sooner I have Lena out of here and someplace where I know the Fox can't reach her, the more relieved I'll be." He squeezed Lena's shoulder.

"We just have to stay alive until the Scorpions arrive," she said. "And right now, a few hours seems like a lifetime." He could tell she felt time was running out for the both of them.

"These guys sure seem capable of finding you no matter what you do. You want some backup?" Henry volunteered. "I can have my men stationed outside the church."

Kyle had considered the idea briefly, but decided

against it. "I don't want to draw any undue attention to the church."

Henry nodded. "I get it. Can I give you a lift anyway?"

As much as Kyle would have loved to say yes, arriving at the church in a police car would certainly stand out to anyone watching the place.

He shook his head. "I'll see if James can pick us up so we're not out in the open for long. We don't know how many more of Alhasan's men might be around."

Henry nodded. "You'll need extra ammo for your weapons…just in case." He went over to his car and brought back extra ammunition.

"Thanks, Henry," Kyle said and shook his hand.

"Be careful. If you need us before your guys arrive, let me know. I can have men there in nothing flat."

Lena couldn't stop shaking. After what just happened, she was terrified Alhasan and his men would find them before they could escape the area.

Kyle must have felt her trembling, because he tugged her closer. "We're going to be okay. This is almost over."

He typed a quick text message to the pastor. The response was quick. "He's going to pick us up in ten minutes in the alley behind the bakery. I think that's just a little ways up on our left."

Kyle seemed preoccupied as they covered the distance quickly and she didn't understand. Was something wrong? He held her so tight, as if he was terrified he'd lose her again.

The pastor was waiting for them behind the bakery.

"Boy, am I glad to see you," Kyle said with a smile.

"And I'm glad you're both alive," James told them. "It

was a terrible thing about Tracy. I can't believe she was working for those people."

In the end, Tracy had proved a clever choice to do the Fox's dirty work. She worked for a church and she in no way sent up any red flags. The pastor had no idea how manipulative these people were. "She was pressured by some very bad people. Has there been any news on her condition?" Kyle asked with concern.

James sighed. "She's still critical. They're not sure she'll make it through the night." He opened the back door of the car. "We'd better get you two out of here as quickly as possible."

Lena got in the backseat first and Kyle slid in next to her.

"Stay as low as you can," he told her. "We'll be okay."

Kyle scrunched down in the seat and Lena did the same. He took her hand and held on to it and she was so grateful. Just having him close made her feel safer.

She remembered a time when she'd been fearless. Al-hasan had taken so much from her. Would she ever be that confident woman again?

Kyle seemed to have a way of picking up on her thoughts. "Give it time. You'll get there. You're not alone anymore, Lena. I'm here and I'm not going anywhere."

She struggled to hold her composure. If she lost it now, he'd know something was wrong. She didn't know how to tell him about the baby. Would he ever forgive her? She turned away yet could feel the questions in him.

James put the car in Drive and pulled out onto the street. "It doesn't look like we're being followed," he said after glancing in the rearview mirror.

"Good. Just do your best to watch for anyone follow-ing too closely," Kyle instructed.

"We're almost there," the pastor informed them a little while later. "It's just about another mile to the church."

Kyle gently touched her face and turned her to face him. "It's going to be okay. As soon as the chopper can get airborne, the team will be on their way. Even allowing for refueling, this is almost over, Lena. We'll get through it together."

Tears filled her eyes and she looked away. She'd give anything to believe that was going to happen, but he didn't know everything and she was terrified he'd hate her when he did.

The car turned into the church parking lot and slowed to a stop. "We're here."

Kyle eased to a sitting position and glanced around. "Let's get inside as quickly as possible. It doesn't look as if anyone is watching the church, but then again, they are highly trained professionals."

He clasped her hand and helped her out. His arms circled her shoulders as they rushed inside and quickly locked the door.

"There's an annex that has a couple of sofas, which are kind of comfortable," James said with a grin. "Food's in the fridge. Help yourself to whatever you want." He led them to a room down the hall from the sanctuary.

"Thanks, James." Kyle smiled in appreciation. "I'm sorry to put you in the middle of this, but we're grateful for your help."

"That's no problem. It's my job and I'm happy to do it. Can I do anything else for you folks?"

Kyle glanced over at Lena. She knew she'd grown quiet and he was trying to understand the change in her.

"We'll be fine," he said. "I think what we need most is rest."

"I can imagine. It looks as if you two haven't had much of that lately. I'll leave you alone. I'll be in my office if you need me."

"Thanks again," Kyle said and waited until the man closed the door and they were alone.

He came over to where she was and drew her close, his hands smoothing the hair from her face.

"How are you holding up?" he asked with his love for her shining in his eyes.

She loved him so much. She didn't want to think about losing him. He'd always been there for her, and she'd put a mission before him and their life together.

"I'm fine," she managed in a shaky voice. "Just ready for this to be over."

She stepped away and he reluctantly let her go. A frown furrowed his brow. "What's wrong? Talk to me, babe. You know you can tell me anything."

If only she could believe he meant that. She was so frightened everything she'd gained again would be lost.

"It's just that Alhasan told me Joseph was dead," she said, grasping the first thing to come to mind. Kyle deserved the truth, yet she just didn't know how to tell him.

He relaxed a little. "We don't know that for sure. Alhasan was probably lying to try to get to you. We'll find him."

He brought her close and kissed her fervently for a moment. "I'm just so happy to have you back, babe," he whispered brokenly against her lips. "So happy I have you again. We're blessed and I love you so much."

He doesn't know everything, her conscience taunted. Would he still want her? She didn't think she could forgive herself for what happened. How could she ask him to do what she was incapable of doing? Where did that leave them?

She wrapped her arms around his waist and held him close, drinking in the familiar scent of him. She ran her fingers through this chestnut hair. In the past, he'd worn it cut short, but it still felt the same against her skin. The warmth in those gray eyes confirmed everything he told her was true. He wanted her.

Kyle was strong and handsome and she would love him for the rest of her life.

"I love you, too, Kyle. With all my heart, no matter what happens, please know that I love you, too."

ELEVEN

He felt as if he were losing her again. She still held something back and it was driving him crazy. Why couldn't she trust him completely?

She sat staring into space, lost and wounded. Her emotional scars deep. The ending of this thing would be just the beginning for her. It might take years to find their way back to where they were before she disappeared. She needed his love and patience. When she was ready, she'd tell him what was wrong. But first they had to survive.

It was as if he could hear the clock ticking away every second that stood between them and safety.

His heart swelled with renewed love while his protective instincts sharpened. With the Fox's true identity still unknown and Alhasan and his men roaming the area looking for them, he prayed for a quick end to the nightmare.

Kyle sat next to her and clasped her hands. She glanced his way. He knew something bad was coming. A storm on the way. It was there in her troubled eyes. His mind flew in a dozen different disturbing directions.

Please don't let it be bad.

"I love you, Lena," he whispered. He'd give anything to be able to hold on to the happiness he felt right now.

A soon as the words were out, she shut down before his eyes.

"What's troubling you, babe?" he implored and prayed she'd tell him the truth.

She shook her head. She wasn't ready yet.

"How is Emily doing?" she asked, the question surprising him. She wanted to know about his sister. But then again, she and Emily had been close.

He forced a smile. "Good. She's attending Harvard, believe it or not. She's studying criminal justice. She told me she wants to be just like you."

She looked down at their joined hands. The wall firmly in place now. "I can't believe she's grown. She was just a teenager when…"

He gathered her close. "This is going to be the happiest day in the world for her. She's missed you, Lena. She reminds me so much of you. She's strong. Independent. Focused."

At one time all those things had driven her to succeed. Not anymore. Lena was a changed woman.

"I can't wait to see her again," she said in a modest tone so unlike Lena.

He could see she was struggling. "I know it's hard. You just need time. This has to be overwhelming for you. Let me help you through it. Don't shut me out."

He squeezed her shoulder and got to his feet. "I'll be right back. I'm going to see if the storm has lifted yet. Hopefully, Jase will have some good news," Kyle told her, but she didn't respond.

He stepped out of earshot but didn't make the call. As happy as he was to have her back, he didn't think he could bear it if he lost her again, even if it was to her own disturbing past.

He closed his eyes and prayed a desperate prayer. *God, she needs You to give her the courage to tell me what's troubling her. Please help her.*

Kyle stood with phone in hand, his thoughts deeply unsettled, when the object in his hand rang unexpectedly. He didn't recognize the number.

Immediately he was on alert. "Who is this?"

"It's me." He recognized Liz's muffled voice. Right away two things became abundantly clear. Liz was hurt and she was in trouble.

"Are you all right? Where are you? I've been trying to reach you for days. Dalton and Booth are searching for you." Silence prompted him to ask, "Liz, are you there?"

"Yes, I'm here." Her voice was barely recognizable. "I have to talk very quietly because they might hear me."

His thoughts orbited. Uneasiness permeated every pore of his body. Something bad had happened.

"We were ambushed—I'm not sure how long ago— while chasing a lead Michael found through monitoring Alhasan's website. He thought it might help us find where Alhasan was holding Sam and his men, only we were attacked. We didn't stand a chance. There were so many. They knew we were coming, Kyle," she said in an ominous tone.

Unbelievable. They'd lured Liz and Michael into a carefully laid trap. The only question was by whom? He remembered what Lena had told him about Alhasan wanting her to take out the entire Scorpion team. He had to find a way to save his people.

"Did you get a good look at the men who took you?" he asked, hoping she could identify someone.

"No, we were hit from behind. We'd just entered the burned-out building Michael identified from one of the photos. They knocked us out. I'd hidden a burner in the lining of my boot. Somehow, they didn't find it. I'm not sure how, because they searched us carefully."

She paused and then said, "I only have a second before they return. I overheard them talking about going to pick up a shipment of weapons. They left a couple of men on guard outside. Sam and his team were here with us, but they were taken away. I'm concerned, Kyle. I haven't seen them since." She paused for a breath. Liz was trying to give him as much information as possible. "There's four other people being held captive with us. An older couple and a man who appears to be in his thirties and a child."

A child. Was it Joseph? Who were the couple and man, and how did they fit with Alhasan's plans? "Do you have any idea where you are being held?" Kyle asked.

The length of time it took for her to answer was disconcerting. "Liz?"

She breathed out a sigh. "Sorry, I thought I heard someone coming. I'm not sure where we are. We've been moved several times and we were in the air for hours. I overheard one of the men mention something about Pennsylvania. When we arrived here, they blindfolded us, but I managed to sneak a peek. I think we're at an abandoned lumber mill."

Pennsylvania! How had the Fox managed to get Liz and Michael into the United States without being detected? Unless he had someone with enough authority to transport them through all the necessary checkpoints? The idea itself was chilling.

Lena had said the Fox was moving his organization to a place called Cedar Creek, and there was a Cedar

Creek near the Pennsylvania border. There was no way this was a coincidence.

He was positive the lumber mill would be near the small town of Cedar Creek. Everything was starting to fall into place. Was the lumber mill the Fox's new head-quarters?

Because he couldn't get what Lena had said to him about the real Fox being an American out of his head, he asked, "Is one of your captors an American?"

Liz hesitated. "No, I don't think so. They were all speaking Dari... Why?" she asked, clearly confused by the question, then she whispered frantically. "Hang on." A lengthy pause followed and then she returned. "Sorry."

Kyle hurriedly told her what Lena had said about the Fox being an American.

"We were so certain Alhasan was the Fox," she said in shock. "I'm not sure if one of them is American. There's only one man who's spoken to us and... Oh, no, some-one's coming. If they catch me with the phone, they'll kill me."

"Liz, hide the phone somewhere, but leave it on so that we can trace it. We'll find you. Until then, stay safe."

There was no answer and he prayed she'd heard, other-wise they'd have no way to find them. He disconnected the call and prayed for their safety.

Kyle quickly updated Jase on what happened.

"I'll put a trace on the burner right away. If it's still on, we can find them. What I don't understand is if they're trying to take out the entire team, then why not just do it? They have two of our people. What's the holdup?"

Kyle had considered the same thing. There had to be a reason. "My guess is he needs something. That's why he's keeping them alive." He just couldn't imagine what.

"Hurry, Jase. We both know the second they locate the phone, they'll pull out of the area. And Liz and Michael's lives will be in jeopardy."

She kept replaying Alhasan's words over in her head. *I should have known you wouldn't follow through with the plan. You're too loyal to the cause...and him. That's why we had to keep track of you.*

He'd been watching her every move since she and Kyle landed in Mountain Song...but how? *That's why we had to keep track of you...*

She slowly got to her feet. There could be only one way. He'd planted a tracking device on her person. Her heart thundered. If that was the case, then what was stopping Alhasan and his men from finding them here?

She had to tell Kyle. She turned toward him. Right away he noticed something was wrong.

"What is it?" he ask when he rushed to her side.

"He's been tracking me somehow."

Puzzled, he didn't understand. "What do you mean?"

"Alhasan. In the car, he told me he knew I would never follow through with the plan. He said that's why he had to keep track of me."

Kyle covered his eyes with his hand. "He planted a tracking device on you. That would explain why they keep finding us. The only question is where? I checked the necklace. There's no device. You didn't bring anything else with you..." He stopped, the look in his eyes frightening.

"What?"

"The only other option is that he's planted it under your skin somewhere." He shook his head. "I should have thought of this. The Fox has long used tracking devices to keep account of his people."

She thought about all the cruelty Alhasan had put her through. This was just another part of it.

"It could be anywhere," Kyle said. "We figured out too late that several of the people the Fox used to do his dirty work had been implanted with tracking devices. Wherever it is, we have to find it fast. It won't take them long to locate us here otherwise."

She nodded and held up her arms, and Kyle ran his fingers lightly over her skin. "Nothing." On a hunch, he examined a spot on her left shoulder.

At one time, she'd had a small birthmark there. Now the spot was covered with a reddish scar.

"This is it," he said and their gazes locked. The second he pressed the spot, she could feel the hard object beneath the skin. Another cruel twist by Alhasan. He'd taken away every means of identifying her in hopes that she would betray the man she loved.

"We have to get it out quickly," she said. "They could be on their way here now."

Kyle agreed. "It's going to hurt. I'll see if I can find a first-aid kit or something to at least clean the wound." He went over to the kitchen area and rummaged through the cabinets until he found a knife and some napkins.

"This is the best I could do," he told her. "The knife is at least sharp. I'm sorry. There's no gentle way to do this."

She just wanted it out. "I know." She clenched her fists and braced for the pain.

The knife tore into her skin and she clamped her teeth down hard on her bottom lip. She'd gotten good at managing pain. This was nothing compared to what she'd gone through.

"Are you okay?" Kyle asked in concern.

"Yes, just get it out. I don't want it inside me any longer."

Working skillfully, Kyle removed the device as quickly as possible, then covered the wound with the napkin. "It's not too bad. It was implanted just beneath the skin."

She kept pressure on the napkin while Kyle smashed the tiny device into pieces.

"All this time, he's been aware of our every move. Do you think they know we're here?"

His silence was as unsettling as it was frightening.

As if in answer to her question, she heard a noise coming from outside. It sounded like multiple cars screeching to a halt close by.

She looked at Kyle. "What was that?"

"I don't know." He barely got the words out when James rushed in.

"There's at least half a dozen vehicles outside. I saw them pull up without their lights. They're outside the sanctuary, as well. What do we do?" James asked in a panic.

She couldn't believe it. She searched Kyle's troubled face. "We're too late."

"I tried calling Henry the second I realized they were out there. The phone's dead," the pastor said in a fearful tone.

Kyle pulled out his cell phone. "There's no service. They're blocking the signal again."

"They want to make sure no one comes to assist. Is there another way out?" she asked James.

He shook his head. "Just through the sanctuary. And the way we came in."

"We can't stay here. Those men will storm the church.

We can't hold them off forever. They'll kill us." She'd fought too hard to die like this.

Kyle touched her arm. "Hey, we have to keep trying. We can't let them win. We're not dead yet. Let's keep fighting."

She'd hold it together for him. "You're right. We can't give up." She turned to James. "Do you have anything we can use as weapons?"

The pastor thought about it for a second. "There's only the kitchen knives and maybe some old boards in the basement."

Lena went to the kitchen and took out every knife that looked strong enough to be deadly.

"Let's get to the basement. At least it will be some-place where we can fortify our surroundings. Make it harder for them to reach us," Kyle said. He was trying so hard to be strong and not let her give up.

James seemed shell-shocked. It took him a second to respond. "Right. It's this way." He stepped out into the hall and headed away from the sanctuary.

"Hang on a second, James. I want to check something out." Kyle slipped into the pastor's office and peered out the window. Lena went with him. "They've surrounded the church. They brought enough manpower to invade a small village."

She met Kyle's gaze. She could see it in his eyes. He didn't like their chances of surviving.

"What are they planning? If they open up with that kind of firepower, they'll have the police here in minutes," she said.

"Probably, but it will be too late for us. It'll be night-fall soon. Our only hope is to hold them off as long as we can."

He dragged James's office chair out and propped it against the door. "Let's make them work for it anyway. If we can secure the basement, maybe once the fireworks start we can hold our ground until the police arrive. James, is the church sanctuary locked?"

"Yes. I locked it before I went to pick you up."

"Good. Let's get to the basement. Lead the way."

James nodded. "The entrance is beneath the stairs leading to the baptistery. It's kind of hidden."

James pulled the door open and flipped on the light switch and they hurried down the rickety stairs. The walls around them seeped moisture. It was at least ten degrees cooler as they descended. The room itself showed signs of decay. This had to be part of the original church.

"We need to secure that door somehow," Kyle said. He looked around for something to use and spotted what looked like an old altar. "That will work. Let's move this in front of the door."

It took all three of them to lift the weighty altar and maneuver it up the stairs.

"That will buy us a little time at least." Kyle glanced around the room. There were no windows. The place was dark except for a single lightbulb. At the back of the room, a wall had been boarded over, the wood rotting in places.

"What's beyond that wall?" Kyle pointed to it.

"I can't believe I almost forgot the passage," the pastor declared as he smacked his forehead.

Kyle and Lena stared at each other and then Lena asked, "What passage?"

"Years ago, this church was part of the Underground Railroad," James told them. "A secret tunnel was dug to transport slaves to their freedom up north. It's been boarded up for years, though."

Lena couldn't believe it. It was like an answer straight from God. "This might be our only chance. We need to get that wall opened up. Do you have hammers, a crowbar, anything we can use to pry the wood from the wall?"

James thought for a second. "Yes, I think we do. A few years back we had to repair part of the sanctuary. The workers left some of their supplies behind." He went over to a pile of boards covered in dust. "Here." he held up a hammer. "It looks like there's only one."

"I'll see if I can find something else," Lena told them as Kyle took the hammer and began to pry some of the boards away.

Lena searched around the room until she found a steel bar the workers had used. She joined Kyle and pried one of the boards with all her strength. It pulled away. Some of the others crumbled in her hands. They'd obviously been rotting away for the years.

Upstairs, a noise sounded like something crashing through the door.

"That sounds like the back door," James said uneasily.

Breaking glass followed and what sounded like a door being ripped from its hinges.

"They're breaking into the sanctuary," James said in amazement. He had no idea how ruthless these men could be.

Lena stopped to listen for a second and heard multiple footsteps rushing into the building.

"They're inside. They'll figure out we're down here soon enough," she said in an urgent tone.

Kyle yanked another board free and there was just enough room to squeeze into the tunnel.

Overhead someone yelled. "Search the entire building. They're still here somewhere. Find them."

"We have to hurry," Kyle urged.

With her heart pounding in her chest, she and James followed close behind Kyle.

"James, do you have any idea where this ends up?" Lena asked as they raced down the narrow tunnel, cobwebs snatching at their faces.

"I'm not sure. I've read some of the old church records, but it was never clear. I think it may be deep in the woods beyond the church."

Kyle flipped on his flashlight app. The tunnel had just enough room for one person stooped over to make it through. As they hurried down it, the vibration from their footsteps dislodged rocks and ancient mortar.

"This whole thing could collapse on us at any moment." Lena shoved aside the disturbing thought of being buried alive.

Something slammed against the basement door.

"They're trying to break down the basement door. We don't have much time," she said with urgency.

They'd barely covered a handful of steps when what sounded like a massive explosion shook the tiny space and a cloud of dust belched past them.

Kyle quickly turned to Lena and tucked her close as air thick with dust covered each of them and made it next to impossible to breathe normally.

Lena coughed violently and wiped streaming tears from her eyes. Up ahead, a wall of rubble now blocked the passage. Part of the tunnel had collapsed upon itself. Unless they could clear the debris quickly, the only way out was the way they'd come. They'd be walking straight into the arms of the men chasing them.

Kyle stared at the rubble in shock. "We've got to clear that. They probably heard the explosion by now. We'll be trapped otherwise."

They began shoving rocks and mortar aside as quickly as possible.

Above them, the door finally gave way and voices could be heard. "They're getting away." Several rounds of shots ricocheted off the walls.

"Hurry, we can squeeze through this way," Kyle said when he barely missed a direct hit.

They had to get down on their hands and knees to clear the minute open space. Kyle waited until both Lena and James were safe before slipping through the narrow opening. Then he shoved as many rocks into the opening as he could before clicking off the flashlight. He didn't want to give their pursuers an advantage.

"There's a light up ahead." He pointed in the direction and they stumbled toward the light, only to find the exit was boarded up.

Lena glanced behind them as flashlights bounced off the unstable structure. The men were gaining on them. "They've reached the rubble. We'll be trapped unless we can get those boards off quickly."

Through the silty light Kyle saw something. "Hold on. It looks as if it's boarded up from the outside. If we kick hard enough, it might break through."

It took precious time before the rotted boards finally gave way.

"They've found the way out. Stop them," one of the men behind them yelled.

Kyle stepped through the opening first and pulled Lena through, followed by James as another round of shots flew past their heads.

"Where are we, James?" he asked in a tight voice.

"Close to my house, I think." James pointed off to the right. "If we can get there, we can call for help."

As they raced through the woods, Lena glanced over her shoulder. Four flashlights scanned the area they'd just left. Who knew how many more men were out there waiting for them.

They reached the house, but Kyle stopped James before he opened the door. "Do you have a car?"

James nodded. "Yes, it's in the garage."

"We need to borrow it. Lock the door and call the cops. Don't let anyone in. Do you have a gun?"

"Yes," the pastor assured him in a frightened tone. "I use it for hunting."

"If anyone tries to break in, shoot to kill."

James punched the garage door opener. "The keys are in it."

"Thanks. We'll leave it someplace where you can find it soon. Stay safe, James."

"You, too. I'll pray for you both," James said before he closed the door and slid the lock in place.

Lena got into the car along with Kyle. He fired the engine and shoved it in Reverse. The car screamed down the drive as the men emerged from the woods.

"Duck," he yelled as a round of bullets riddled the side of the car.

Kyle swerved with the impact but managed to keep it on the drive. The men continued firing as they chased after them on foot. Once Kyle reached the end of the drive, he made a hard right then sped down the road.

Lena glanced behind. She could see the men heading for the house. "Do you think James will be okay?"

Kyle looked in the rearview mirror. "I hope so. These

men are ruthless. We have to get out of here. They'll call for backup. Block the roads out of town. We can't afford to get caught. There are too many lives at stake." He told her that two of his team members had been taken hostage by Alhasan. They were being held at an abandoned lumber mill near the Pennsylvania border.

Lena's thoughts raced. Was Alhasan using the captives to draw them out? "We have to save them."

Kyle didn't answer right away, and she knew there was more. "There are others being held hostage, as well. An older couple, a man...and a boy."

She jerked his way. "It has to be Joseph. He's alive."

He nodded. "Do you have any idea who the older couple and the man are?" he asked.

She couldn't imagine. "I have no idea. Joseph was the only one at the prison I know about."

He drove in silence for a long time. "For a little bit, when you first told me the other woman was Lena..." He stopped and shook his head. "Well, I thought the child might be mine...ours," he admitted. "These last few days have been a roller-coaster ride."

Suddenly, it was hard to breathe. She remembered... something. About the baby. Her little girl. Alhasan had told her the child was dead at birth but she remembered... a cry. Had he taken her daughter's life? She covered her trembling mouth with her hand before the sob escaped, but Kyle had seen her pain.

"Lena?"

She couldn't look at him. She loved him so much and he was so happy to have her back.

"Babe, you can tell me anything. I know what you went through at that prison was horrible, and I can't comprehend how much you've suffered. I just wish that I hadn't settled for what was before my eyes."

Curious, she glanced his way. "What do you mean?"

"I mean it never felt as if you were gone. Even after we found the body in the desert with your ring, I didn't feel like I'd lost you in here." He pointed to his chest. "I should have kept searching. I shouldn't have settled. I'm so sorry."

He was apologizing to *her*. He'd done everything within his power to find her. The evidence was deliberately stacked to make Kyle and the CIA believe she was dead. He was innocent. She was not.

She was the bad person here. Not Kyle. "You didn't know. It's not your fault, Kyle. You did everything you could. Alhasan and the Fox wanted you to believe I was dead."

Lena thought about the time before her capture. The village in which she had been embedded had been crackling with tension in the days before the attack. The family she stayed with was terrified she would be discovered as CIA.

And then the attack happened. The family murdered before her eyes. She'd been badly injured and struggling to live. Her memory shot. The village leveled. They'd spared her. Now she knew it was deliberate. She was a key ingredient in the Fox's plan.

"We need to stay out of sight as much as possible," Kyle told her. "They'll be looking for this car." He hesitated and she could tell something was troubling him. "Best case scenario, it will be hours before Aaron can fly the team here if the storm lifts quickly. That's a lifetime when you're dealing with the Fox. He could move Liz and the others before we have the chance to rescue them.

And once he believes they've served their purpose, he'll kill them." He glanced her way. "I have to go after them."

She understood. You didn't leave a man behind. "I'm coming with you."

He immediately rejected the idea. "I can't lose you again, Lena. I won't."

She sat up straighter and prepared for battle. "I'm coming, Kyle. I can help. I promised Joseph I wouldn't let anything happen to him, and I'm not about to go back on that promise."

TWELVE

The woman beside him had grown increasingly distant with every mile they covered. Kyle's mind went crazy thinking about the possibilities of what she kept to herself. Did she blame him for not doing more to find her? She said she understood, but she'd suffered dearly at Al-hasan's hands. Would some part of her blame him still?

He replayed his earlier conversation with Liz. Something had been different in her voice. He'd seen Liz in some hairy situations before, and her strength was unshakable. Uncertainty was out of character for her and yet there was no denying the uneasiness in her tone.

What he didn't understand was how someone as obviously smart as the Fox wouldn't find the cell phone Liz had tucked in her boot. More to the point, if one of his goals was to take out the rest of the Scorpions, then why not just kill Liz and Michael...unless they were part of his team?

He kept remembering what Lena had said about the true person in charge being an American. What if she was wrong? Could the true Fox be a woman? Liz was certainly intelligent enough to mastermind such an operation, but the thought of her betraying them was impossible, surely. Still, he'd had a feeling she was trying to warn him of something. The only question was what?

He glanced over at Lena. She hadn't said so much as a handful of words. He clasped her hand. "Talk to me. Tell me what's troubling you. Please tell me you forgive me for failing you."

A sob escaped. "Oh, Kyle. I don't blame you. I blame me."

This was the last thing he expected. "Why would you blame yourself? You did nothing wrong."

She laughed, but there was no humor in it or her face. "That's not true. I did so much wrong." She shifted a little so that she could see him clearly. The desperation in her eyes was hard to take. "Kyle, I was pregnant when I went on that final mission. I found out the day I was scheduled to leave. By then it was too late. We didn't have time to find a replacement and the mission was too essential to scrub."

In a second, his heart shattered into a thousand pieces. He jerked the car over to the side of the road and put it in Park. He couldn't make it make sense. "Why? Why would you do that?"

Tears filled her eyes. "Because I thought what we were doing was important. The mission was critical. At the time, we had no idea how critical. There was no time to change the plan. The people I would be staying with were anxious enough as it was. If we tried to put someone else in at the last minute, it could have caused the entire thing to fall apart."

His resentment rose like bile. "You were pregnant when you went on that mission and you didn't tell me. You put your life and our child's in jeopardy for a mission?"

She said something, but he was beyond hearing her. He was devastated by the news. "You should have told me. It was my child, too. I deserved to be part of the decision. You had no right to shut me out."

She looked so grief stricken and yet he couldn't think of anything but what she'd done to them. All these years he hadn't known he was going to be a father.

"You're right," she said and he barely caught the words. "I should have told you. I wanted to, but you were so against me going on any missions those last few years. Taking risks. I didn't know how to tell you, and I didn't think it was possible to pull out at that late hour."

She was right. In the years before she disappeared, he'd had a terrible feeling every single time she left on a mission. His gut twisted into knots. He couldn't eat. It was as if time was running out and he couldn't bear the thought. Still, he wasn't ready to accept his part just yet.

"There's more," she said. He stared straight ahead unable to look at her. His hands grew clammy. "Kyle, I gave birth to a girl. Alhasan told me the baby died, but I think he killed her."

He felt as if someone had dropped a ton of bricks on him. It was too much to bear. Alhasan had murdered their innocent baby girl. The walls of the car became claustrophobic and he desperately needed air. Needed to pray before he said something he would regret forever. Needed God's peace.

He reached for the door handle.

"Where are you going?" she sobbed.

"I can't deal with this now. I need to be alone. Don't follow me," he said without looking at her.

He was barely aware of her calling his name. He stumbled from the car and began walking. He had to put distance between himself and Lena. He'd never experienced an anger so great before, not even for the Fox, and to have it directed at the woman he loved was almost too much to take. He stopped at the edge of the woods close to the road.

What she said threatened to destroy all of his hope for their future together. They had a child. Lena's fateful decision had resulted in their child's death. He couldn't wrap his mind around that truth.

He dropped to his knees and prayed for comfort, but this was the one time answers were hard to come by.

Kyle could feel himself shutting down emotionally. He couldn't deal with this now and finish what needed to be done.

Slowly, he got to his feet and scrubbed away the tears. Then he went back to the car, got in and put it in Drive. He pulled back onto the road, still without looking at Lena. He could feel her watching him in the darkness and yet he couldn't talk to her.

He was inconsolable. To keep from going crazy, Kyle dissected every word of Liz's story. Even if he bought the Fox's men had overlooked the phone, he didn't understand why they'd risk being caught by transporting two missing CIA agents into the United States. Unless he needed something from them.

Hadir had said Alhasan was grooming a woman for a mission that would shock the world. What if Hadir's intel had been wrong? What if Liz was the true Fox and Alhasan and the American were working for her?

"Kyle…"

His hands tightened on the wheel. A single muscle worked in his jaw. "I can't do this now, Lena. I can't talk about this with you and not lose it. Let's just concentrate on what we have to do. Because right now, I'm not sure if I'll ever be able to forgive you for what you've done."

His phone rang. Lena couldn't help but take every second of his silence as a rejection.

"Okay, thanks" she heard him say before he disconnected the call.

He spared her a glance. "That was Jase. We have a location for the phone. Liz was right. It's a lumber mill outside Cedar Creek, Pennsylvania." He sounded so distant. Her biggest fear was that her own foolishness had sealed their future.

"We can be there in two hours. We'll sit on the place until Jase and the team arrive."

"Okay," she said and hated that they sounded like strangers talking to each other.

She noticed him glancing in the rearview mirror.

"What is it?" She turned and saw a car's headlights still some distance away. Someone was behind them. "Is it them?"

The uneasiness in his eyes did little to reassure her. "I don't know, but we can't take the chance. We need to get off this road until they've passed." He killed the lights and squinted through the windshield. "There's a hill up ahead to the right. If we can make it over, we can use it as cover."

He gripped the wheel tight and floored the gas. Lena hung on to the door with all her might as they topped the hill. What looked like someone's pasture spread out before them. Off to the right, there was a clump of small trees. Kyle pulled the car behind them and stopped.

He pointed back the way they'd come. A line of brush separated the hill from the road. "If we can slip over there, we should have enough camouflage to keep them from seeing us. We'll have the element of surprise if they attack."

He didn't look at her as he asked, "Are you ready?"

Her heart was breaking. She felt as if the chance they'd had at a future was slipping away with every moment he refused to talk to her. If they survived those men behind them, if they were able to capture the Fox and end this thing once and for all, what then?

She cleared her throat. It was next to impossible to answer, but she did. "Yes, I'm ready."

When they reached the brush, Lena could make out the road below in the moonlight. The car was almost right on top of them now.

The men inside had the windows down and a spotlight searching the area where Kyle and Lena knelt. They both ducked.

"I told you there was no one here," one of the men said.

"And I'm telling you I saw car lights ahead of us." A second man's voice, clearly agitated that his partner doubted him.

The spotlight homed in on the area where they were hiding, and Lena held her breath. "See? Nothing. You're being paranoid and we're out of time. We have work to do. Let's go."

The partner didn't answer, but the spotlight disappeared and the car's speed picked up.

"Let's follow them. They could lead us to where the hostages are being held," Kyle said.

They raced back to the car and Kyle put it in Drive, still without any lights.

"We can't afford to have them spot us. We'll have to hang back a little ways. At least there's some moonlight, otherwise it would be near impossible to manage this winding road."

Kyle kept a safe distance while the car ahead seemed oblivious to their tail. After they'd followed the car for more than an hour, it slowed down and turned off.

"This isn't right. We're heading the wrong way," he said in concern. "The lumber mill is still some distance from here."

She stared at the fading taillights. "Where do you think they're going?"

Kyle shook his head. "I don't know. Maybe they've moved the hostages already."

The car made another right-hand turn and Kyle braked just short of the exit.

Lena peered through the opening. "It looks like a private drive."

"We'll have to follow on foot. We can't risk them seeing us." He tucked the car out of sight and got out as quietly as possible. She did the same.

The drive was barely wide enough for a small vehicle, and it wound around in snakelike fashion.

When it suddenly ended, Kyle tapped her arm and they slipped behind some trees.

The two men they'd followed were standing outside their car talking to a couple of others.

Lena could just make out what they were saying.

"You're late. We should have left half an hour ago. The schedule's been moved forward."

"We were delayed because of *them*. We're here now." Lena recognized the man's voice from earlier.

"We need to get the last of the weapons on the truck and en route right away, otherwise…" The man didn't finish, but the implication was deadly. The men headed for what looked like a military transport truck.

"We have to stop them from moving those weapons," Kyle told her.

"There could be other men here. What do you want to do?" she asked.

"We need something to act as a diversion. Can you cover me? I'm going to drive their car straight into that truck."

Lena shoved her fear for Kyle's safety down deep. She had to stay focused. "Yes, I've got you."

Something softened in his expression just for a second before the hard edge returned.

"You won't have much time after I start the car before they open fire."

"I've got you, Kyle," she assured him.

And she did. She wouldn't waver. She'd be there for him even if it cost her life. She loved him that much.

They eased to the car and Kyle hopped into the driver's seat and tucked down low. The second he started the car, the men jerked around and Lena opened fire.

Kyle put the vehicle in Drive and headed for the truck. The men realized what they were doing and opened fire on Lena full force.

With her walking beside the moving car, using it as cover, the men jumped behind the truck and continued taking shots. When the vehicle was a couple of feet away, Kyle floored the gas and rammed the side of it hard.

Someone screamed. They'd injured one of the men. Lena charged the truck.

"Drop it," she said and three men whirled to face her with their weapons drawn. Out of the corner of her eye she saw Kyle round the back of the truck.

One of the men fired at her. She hit the ground, aimed for the weapon and returned fire. The gun flew from his hands.

The two remaining men slowly lowered their guns and tossed them in front of them. The fourth man, who had taken the brunt of the hit, was unconscious.

Lena grabbed the men's weapons while Kyle knelt beside the unconscious man and felt for a pulse.

"He's alive. I'll call the local law enforcement and have them pick these guys up. From the looks of the smoke coming out of the car's engine, they're not going anywhere. Let's make sure the same can be said for the truck." He shot out all four tires and then did the same to the engine.

"I'll get their phones. We don't want them calling for help before the police arrive." Lena searched the men and retrieved their cell phones while Kyle covered her.

"I'm going to check that shed over there. You got them?" She nodded and he hurried off. There weren't any other buildings around other than the storage shed. Within minutes, Kyle reappeared.

"There're enough US military weapons in there to wage a small war," he told her in disbelief. "If that's what's left to move, I hate to see what's passed through here already."

Lena shook her head in disbelief. "Where are the hostages?" she demanded of the men.

The man closest to her shook his head. "They're not here. We can't help you. He'll kill us if we do."

Instantly, one of his partners rebuked him. "Shut up, you fool."

"Who are you talking about?" Lena moved closer to the first man. "Tell us and we'll help you."

The man shook his head, regretting his outburst.

"I'll ask you again, where are the hostages being held?" she repeated in a deadly serious tone. "If you want to live, you need to cooperate."

"Keep your mouth shut," the partner snarled. "I'm not dying because of you."

The man was clearly not as loyal. His gaze ping-ponged from Kyle to Lena before giving in. "Some are dead. The rest are at the lumber mill. But you're too late. They're leaving tonight. If we don't show soon, they'll know something went wrong and they'll leave without the rest of the weapons."

Lena's heart pounded a traumatic beat. Her worry was all for Joseph. "What about the boy? Is the boy okay?"

The man stared at her for the longest time. "Yes, I think so," he admitted at last.

Relief had her bending over, her hands touching her knees. Alhasan had lied. Joseph was alive.

Just a little longer, Joseph. Hang on, we're almost there.

"Let's get out of here," Kyle told her with the same gruff edge to his voice as before. They were back to square one.

"You can't leave us here. They'll think we're deserters. He'll send people here. We'll be branded as traitors," the man continued pleading. "Please, he'll kill us."

Lena didn't recognize any of the men, which led her to believe they were US recruits. "Not if you do what you're told and stay put. Someone will be here soon to pick you up. If you try anything foolish, you will be dead."

Once they reached the car, Kyle did a U-turn and headed back to the main road.

"Do you think we'll make it in time?" she asked, because she couldn't bear the thought of being so close to saving Joseph and having him perish before they could reach him.

Kyle glanced her way briefly. "I sure hope so."

She closed her eyes. "Father, please don't let us be too late," she prayed under her breath, and Kyle shot her a puzzled look. She understood. When she'd spoken about God in the past, he thought he was dealing with Ella Weiss, a missionary. Now that he knew she was Lena, he probably remembered her lack of faith before, and she could certainly understand his confusion. She hadn't believed in God before she left on the mission. A lot had changed in her life and his. They had a whole lot of obstacles to overcome still, and she wasn't sure where to start.

The silence that permeated the car was discouraging. She clutched her hands together. Maybe it was best this way. She wasn't the woman she'd been before. And Kyle deserved so much more than this shell of a person she'd become.

THIRTEEN

He knew she had questions; he could feel her eyes on him in the darkness. She needed his forgiveness, but he couldn't give it to her just yet.

He couldn't get Liz's conversation out of his head. Something about it bugged him. She'd said Sam was there once but he and his men had been taken away. It wasn't so much what she said but the way she said it. He didn't believe Liz was responsible for betraying the team or Hadir.

She was trying to warn him of something. If Sam and his team hadn't provided anything useful, why bring them all the way to the United States? How was Duncan connected? Was he the real Fox in spite of Tracy's denial? Jase had been able to track Duncan's travels over the last ten years. He'd made only a handful of trips to Afghanistan.

"How many times did you say you saw the American at the prison?" he asked on impulse.

Lena rousted herself from her own dark thoughts. "Maybe six or more times through the years. Why?"

He shook his head. It all seemed just a little too convenient. Lena told him the American had blond hair and blue eyes. Yet Tracy had confirmed Duncan wasn't the man who contacted her and his eyes were brown. Whatever his connection, Kyle was convinced Duncan wasn't the man calling the shots.

An uneasy thought slithered through his head. Sam had blond hair and blue eyes and fit the description Tracy gave him to a T. What if Sam had faked the kidnapping?

Kyle recalled how the chopper hadn't shown any signs of taking fire. It had simply drifted to the ground.

But he knew Sam. The man had been part of the CIA for several years before he decided to go into the private sector. They'd worked missions together.

So who was the Fox? And more important, why was it so important that he gain access to their headquarters? He was after something. No doubt something they didn't realize was important.

Through the information Eddie Peterson had smuggled out of Afghanistan, they'd been systematically tracking down the weapons storage sites until the Fox figured out they had the information and the weapons had been moved. Jase's team had gone over every piece of information in those files. Whatever the Fox was after, it wasn't part of them.

The only things that were kept at the Scorpion headquarters that weren't part of the network system were the agents' personnel files. Anonymity was crucial in their line of work, and they'd learned from past mistakes not to have those files where they could be hacked.

Why would the Fox need the Scorpions' personnel files? He shook his head. The more immediate concern was rescuing the hostages while they were still close by.

They were about fifteen miles from the Pennsylvania border and he was constantly watching the rearview mirror. He couldn't get it out of his head that they might be walking into a setup.

As they drew closer, Kyle's uneasiness for Lena's safety grew. "I don't know what we'll be facing when we get to the lumber mill. I think it's best if I take you to the local police station, where you will be safe."

He didn't get the words out before he had her answer. "No, I'm not letting you do this alone. We both know this could be a trap. We have no idea how many men they have or even who we're after."

"Lena…" Her answer wasn't unexpected, but still.

"I want to bring the Fox to justice just as much as you do. Alhasan has to pay for taking our child's life and for Joseph's mother. There's no time for a detour. You heard those men. We may be too late already. We can't risk them getting away."

The anger in her eyes disturbed him. She'd always been a determined woman, but this went beyond that. He was worried about the past tearing them apart, but what if the anger and bitterness that she'd shoved deep inside her heart was the thing that destroyed her? He couldn't let that happen. No matter where their future lay, whether together or apart, he wasn't about to let the Fox destroy his wife.

In spite of everything, he still loved her. Did they have a chance together? Only God knew.

According to the map of the area Jase had sent, the mill was just up ahead. Kyle killed the lights and parked the car.

"We'll have to go the rest of the way on foot. We don't want to let them know we're coming."

She nodded and they got out of the car.

"It should be about a quarter of a mile that way." He

pointed to an area to the left and started walking. The idea that they were so close to the man they'd been chasing for years made it hard to go slow. Still, the last thing they needed was to tip him off…if they hadn't already.

It was like a snail's pace maneuvering quietly through the thick brush and overgrown trees. Through it all Lena never missed a beat. Eventually the underbrush opened up into a clearing and Kyle held out his arm to block Lena from going any farther.

What looked like a large barn lay straight ahead of them. There were several smaller storage units scattered around.

"I don't like it. This feels off to me," he said, his voice tense. Kyle took out his binoculars and glanced around the area. Nothing moved. He switched the mode to thermal. There was no indication of body heat anywhere around the area. What happened to the hostages?

"Stay behind me. If anything jumps up, find cover fast."

She slowly nodded and they eased from their cover and slowly headed for the largest storage building, with Kyle stopping periodically to listen.

When they reached the building, they eased along the side until they were at the front. The door was wide-open. The hair at the back of his neck stood up, alarming him— something was wrong.

Please protect us, he prayed, then eased through the entrance with Lena close behind. Both weapons drawn.

At first glance, the building appeared to be empty of life and weapons.

Where were Liz and the others? How long had they been moving the weapons from the area? Liz had said she'd overheard them discussing picking up a shipment earlier today. Had they moved them so quickly?

"Are we too late?" Lena asked as they glanced around the cavernous space.

He wasn't so sure. He felt as if they were part of some macabre scene, playing out their parts. "I hope not. Let's search the place. Maybe they left some clue behind." He moved toward some stacked wood in the left corner while Lena went the opposite way.

He spotted the phone tucked on top of the wood as if it were meant to be located. "I found the cell phone." He picked it up. It was still turned on. The battery charge was almost nonexistent.

"Do you think they found it?" Lena came over to him.

"Yes, I believe so." If they'd found the phone, had Liz and Michael paid the ultimate price? His gut told him they'd moved the hostages to a different location. They wouldn't bother to hide the bodies if they'd killed them. The Fox would want Kyle to find them…unless they needed them to think they were still alive so that they'd follow them. Kyle shoved that thought aside.

"I remember seeing an open area on the map. It's not far from here. It could serve as a landing strip."

"What's wrong?" she asked as if reading his unsettled thoughts.

"I'm not sure." He kept replaying the way Sam's chopper went down in his head. Sam's man had said they had been shot, but there didn't appear to be any damage and the chopper was intact when it landed. Was it possible Sam was the real Fox?

On a hunch, Kyle remembered he'd saved an old voice mail message from Sam—a birthday greeting.

"I need you to listen to something," he told her and retrieved the message and held it up for Lena to hear. Her reaction was immediate. The second she heard Sam's voice she recognized it.

"That's him," she exclaimed in horror. "That's the American from the prison. The one in charge. Kyle, that's the Fox."

He couldn't wrap his head around the truth. The man he claimed as a friend, the one he'd broken bread with many times, was really the notorious terrorist who had been systematically trying to take out their team for years. Why? He couldn't understand why Sam would do such a thing. It couldn't be about the money. Working in the private sector paid well, according to Sam.

"Who is he?" she asked when she saw the betrayal on his face.

"A friend. Or at least someone I thought was a friend. Obviously, he was just using me. He's a former CIA agent. I worked with him on the job for several years and even after he started his hostage retrieval business. He'd seen how devastated I was at losing you, and yet he knew you were alive all along. I can't believe he might be the Fox."

Still, it made sense. Kyle recalled little things from his past encounters with Sam that should have served as a warning. Sam had jokingly tried to get the location of the Scorpions' headquarters out of Kyle along with the type of security system they used to protect it. And Sam always managed to be in the same area when something went down with the Fox. In the past, he'd shared information about the Scorpions' hunt for the Fox with Sam, and all the while the man he was searching for might have been right there by his side.

"Did Alhasan ever mention what was so important at the compound that they needed access to it physically?"

Lena shook her head. "No, only that it was critical that I gain access and then…" She looked away.

When they reached the clearing, Kyle stopped and squinted through the trees.

"There's a plane and a helicopter," he said in shock. "Both appear ready to leave at a moment's notice."

"Why do they need both?" Lena asked the obvious question.

"That's a good question. We need that backup now. We can't afford to let them leave the area." He checked his watch. Jase would still be a good hour out. He tried Jase's phone then turned to her in shock.

"The signal's gone. If they're blocking it, they know we're coming. Keep your eyes open. I can't help but feel we're doing exactly what they want us to do."

His hands grew damp with sweat. The hair on the back of his neck stood at attention. "I don't like this." He turned back to her. "Wait here—" He barely got the words out before multiple gunshots split the night sky around them.

"Get back," he yelled and they dived for cover.

"I counted three shooters. They're to the right of us," Lena said.

"If the Fox is on the plane, there's no way they won't know we're here. We won't be able to surprise them."

Lena squatted next to him. "If we can circle around behind the shooters, maybe we can manage to take them by surprise. Find out how many men are on the plane."

He couldn't shake the feeling that they were doing exactly what the Fox expected of them. Still, they had to do everything in their power to save the hostages. "I'll see if I can draw them out here." He nodded toward the open area. "Can you circle behind?"

She got to her feet, reminding him of the old Lena. Before she left he stopped her. "Hang on." She turned to face him and he came to where she stood. There was so much he wanted to tell her, but the hurt inside wouldn't let him just yet. "Be careful," he said instead.

Her disappointment was easy to read. She nodded then jogged through the trees. Kyle stepped out into the clearing for a second and fired in the direction of the shots. Three returned rounds of gunfire blasted past him.

"Hurry, Lena," he whispered as the men firing on him advanced. One cleared the opening and Kyle aimed for his leg. The man yelped in pain then dropped to the ground and grabbed his injured leg. Kyle quickly disarmed him.

Another man opened fire and Kyle ducked deeper into the woods. The man must have thought he had the advantage, because he continued firing as he drew closer. Kyle flattened himself against a tree until the man passed by.

In the distance, Kyle heard a scream followed by what sounded like a scuffle. Lena.

The man advancing paused and turned to look behind him. Kyle took advantage and grabbed the man. He wrapped him in a choke hold and squeezed tight. It felt like an eternity before the man lost consciousness.

"Don't move," Kyle warned the injured man and then raced toward the fight. Before he reached the spot, Lena emerged.

He closed the distance between them. "Are you all right?" he asked and couldn't hide his concern.

"I'm fine. But there's no way they don't know we're coming now."

He couldn't imagine why the Fox's men weren't rushing to the other's aid. The situation screamed setup. "That's why I need to go in alone."

"Kyle…" Always so determined, she was ready to argue her cause.

He couldn't let her this time. She'd suffered enough. If one of them was to die, he wanted it to be him. "I need you to stay here. Keep an eye on these men. If they try anything, shoot them."

She reluctantly agreed. "Okay. Please be careful," she whispered and touched his face tenderly. For the moment he let go of the anger inside and kissed her hand.

"I will." With one final searching look, he moved toward the plane. The engines were running. The plane was ready for takeoff. The chopper's blades were spinning, as well. Both machines could leave at a moment's notice. What were they waiting on?

His uneasiness rose to a crescendo as he slowly moved up the steps to the front entrance of the plane. The door wasn't fully closed. With his survival instincts sharp, he eased through the opening and stopped dead. His worst fears realized.

Right away an armed man drew down on him. "Drop it, Agent Jennings," Peter Duncan ordered. "We've been expecting you."

One question flew through his head. Were both Lena and Tracy wrong? Was Duncan the real Fox? Kyle's impression of the man was he didn't act like someone in authority.

At the middle of the plane, Alhasan had a gun shoved against Liz's temple. Kyle noticed her right arm hung at her side. He'd been right. She was hurt.

"Are you okay?" he asked Liz. He needed to know if she was capable of fighting when it came to that.

She managed a nod before Alhasan dug the gun deeper against her temple and she flinched.

Next to Liz, a seriously injured Michael was bleeding from his side and pale from loss of blood.

Seated just behind Alhasan were an older couple and another younger man. Kyle recognized Ella Weiss's parents and her fiancé right away.

He noticed the child huddled against the window. He appeared to be around six or seven. This had to be Joseph. Something about the boy snatched his full attention. He was so innocent and he looked…

"Glad you made it, Agent Jennings. You fell right in with our plan. I thought you were more intelligent," Alhasan sneered. "Not that it matters. Now that you're here we can leave. She's not cooperating." He waved his weapon at Liz.

Kyle couldn't let that happen. He had to find a way to get the hostages away from Alhasan and his goons.

"The rest of the Scorpions are on their way here now. You're not going anywhere, Alhasan. Give yourself up and things will go easier for you and your men."

Alhasan laughed smugly. "You're right. There is no way out…for you. Even if you kill all of us, there will be more. You can't imagine how many there are. And they're closer than you think," Alhasan said knowingly.

The thought was chilling. Had the Fox embedded his men into the elite Scorpion team?

Minutes passed while her heart tattooed a frantic rhythm and her uneasiness for Kyle grew.

Behind her, she heard someone running through

the bushes. Weapon drawn, she whirled to listen. They weren't coming after her; they were running away. Lena hurried to the man Kyle had shot.

With the Glock trained on his head she asked, "Who's on the plane? Where are they heading?"

The man held his wounded leg and glared at her. "You think I'd help you?" he asked in derision.

"If you don't want to spend the rest of your life in a federal prison then, yes, I do."

"I'd rather be in prison than dead," the man snarled.

Lena moved closer and the man shrank away. He wasn't as brave as he wanted her to believe.

"Is *he* in there?" she asked and the man stared up at her in fear then shook his head.

Lena realized she wasn't going to get anything out of him. "If you know what's best for you, you'll stay put and not move an inch."

With her heartbeat drowning out all sound, she eased toward the plane. Kyle could be in there, hurt. She had to help him. Lena quietly crept up the steps to the back entrance and eased the door open. She slipped inside and stopped to listen for a second. Voices. Kyle and… Alhasan.

Lena flattened against the wall and edged toward the passenger cabin. She spotted Kyle at the front of the plane. Duncan had a gun drawn on him. Midway down, Alhasan was holding the woman who had flown her to the base captive. The second agent Kyle had called Michael appeared seriously injured. Close to the back, an armed man watched the rest of the hostages.

If she could get past the armed man, she'd have a split second to reach Alhasan.

She rushed the man. She slammed the butt of her

Glock against his temple and he dropped to the floor. Kyle lunged for Duncan, catching him off guard. Within seconds, he'd disarmed him.

And then she and Alhasan squared off.

"Drop it, Alhasan, or I promise you won't live to tell of this," she assured him in a deadly serious voice.

Alhasan released Liz and aimed the weapon at Lena. She never wavered. He'd caused her so much pain. She was immune to his threats.

He glared her for the longest time. Was he expecting her to fear him still? Be under his spell?

She stepped closer. "Now, Alhasan," she ordered.

She saw his uncertainty. Something of the rage she felt inside must have gotten through to him, because he slowly lowered the gun.

"You fool. He'll kill us all," Duncan admonished.

"Kick the weapon this way," she told Alhasan, who grudgingly did as she commanded.

Lena noticed Joseph cowering in fear by the older couple. He was scared but physically unhurt. *Thank You, God.*

"Come to me, Joseph." The boy was clearly terrified of Alhasan. "He's not going to hurt you ever again. I need you to come here," she urged. Joseph kept a wide berth between himself and Alhasan as he edged past and ran to her. She knelt down and hugged the boy tight. She could feel him trembling. "It's okay. You're safe now. Get behind me." She stood and Joseph quickly slipped behind her.

As she stared at Alhasan, something deep inside her splintered and the wealth of pain she'd suffered at his hands all came pouring out. She wanted him to pay for what he had done to Joseph and to her. To Kyle and their innocent child. Alhasan was at her mercy now. She could do to him what he'd done to her and no one would stop her. She moved closer, the weapon inches from his face.

"Don't do it, Lena," Kyle urged in a gentle tone that reached through her dark thoughts. "If you kill him, you'll be no better. He's not worth it. We need him."

She couldn't remember seeing Alhasan so frightened. "Please don't kill me," he pleaded with her. "I'll do whatever you want. I'll tell you everything, but please don't kill me." Without his men to back him up, he was just a frightened coward begging for his life.

Lena stared at him for the longest time while desperately praying for the strength to let go of her anger.

She drew in a steadying breath. Kyle was right. If she killed Alhasan, she'd have to live with that action for the rest of her life. She'd already made one mistake that haunted her. She didn't want to live in bitterness and anger any longer. It was time to let it go.

"You're right. He's not worth it," she said finally.

She could feel Joseph's hold tighten on her legs and she lowered the gun. No matter what her future with Kyle might be, she was still alive and Joseph needed her. God had brought her through the nightmare of seven years in prison. It wasn't up to her to make Alhasan pay for his crimes.

FOURTEEN

Kyle let go of the breath he'd held inside. He'd been so afraid she wouldn't listen. He certainly wouldn't blame her if she hadn't.

He watched as Lena knelt next to the boy and held him close, and he was struck again by how familiar the child appeared to him. He didn't understand it. Now was not the time to sort out how. They had to get the hostages off the plane before Sam returned. Kyle was certain he was close.

"Where's Sam?" he asked Liz.

She shook her head. "I don't know. Alhasan's men took Sam and the rest of his team away and I haven't seen them since."

"Is he the one in charge?" he asked point-blank.

She hesitated a little too long. Why was Liz reluctant to talk? In the back of his mind, he recalled Liz telling him that she and Sam had shared a few friendly meals together in the past.

"Liz?" He pressed her for an answer.

"Yes, I think he is. But I still can't believe it. I thought I knew him. He made me call you. Kyle, he has—" Before she could finish, a figure appeared in the doorway close to him. Sam.

Sensing they were in danger, Lena gathered Joseph in her arms and rushed to get him to safety. Before she escaped, the rest of Sam's men entered through the back door and she backed away.

One of the men snatched Joseph from her arms.

"No," she screamed and lunged for the man. A second man grabbed her arm and shoved a knife close to her side.

"Drop your weapon, Kyle. It's over for you." Sam's smile held an ugly edge to it. This was not the man he'd once considered a friend. The ruthless expression on Sam's face all but assured Kyle he was now face-to-face with the true Fox.

"You couldn't leave it alone, could you?" Sam smirked with bitterness and shook his head. "If you'd just left things alone, none of this would be necessary."

Sam moved to within inches of a visibly shaken Alhasan. "And you, such a miserable failure, my friend."

Alhasan's mouth opened and closed several times before he could answer. "No, I didn't tell them anything, I promise. I didn't tell them about you. I wouldn't betray you."

"Shut up," Sam ordered, but Alhasan continued to plead his case.

"I promise, I didn't. I've remained loyal to you through all these years. Haven't I proved myself enough? I had Abby, the woman I loved, killed for you. You were afraid she'd crack when the Scorpions interrogated her, so I sacrificed my happiness for you. I've proved my loyalty. I would never betray you."

Sam didn't listen. He aimed the weapon at Alhasan's

head. "I'm sorry, my friend, but you've outlived your usefulness."

"No, please, no," Alhasan pleaded and backed away, his hands in front of him.

Sam fired once at close range, instantly killing Alhasan.

Stunned, Kyle still couldn't believe this was the same man he knew. His trusted friend was the one they'd been searching for all along. It was Sam who had ultimately been responsible for Lena's capture and the death of their child.

Anger sped through every fiber of his body. Acting on it alone, Kyle charged Sam before he could get a shot off. He knocked the weapon from Sam's hand, grabbed his shoulders and slugged him hard. As they scuffled back and forth, Kyle was vaguely aware of Liz grabbing the gun Sam had lost.

While Kyle tried to gain the upper hand, Lena jammed her elbow into side of the man holding her. Freed, she charged for Joseph, but the man with the knife slashed at her. She screamed and immediately grabbed her side as blood oozed through her shirt.

"No," Kyle yelled and finally freed himself from Sam's hold. Terrified he'd lose her again, he tried to reach her side, but one of Sam's men stuck a gun at Kyle's head while another shoved Liz's injured arm and she fell to her knees.

"Are you okay?" Kyle asked Lena. She tried to be strong, but he could see she was losing blood. He couldn't lose her. Not like this. Not with his anger standing between them.

"As I said, you should have left things alone," Sam muttered and turned to Duncan. "Take those two with us." He nodded to Liz and Michael. One man jerked Liz to her feet while another forced a visibly weak Michael from the plane.

While the man strong-armed Liz past him, her gaze held his briefly. Was she trying to tell him something or... Was she working with Sam?

Why would he need her and Michael? Only three people had access to the code to unlock the safe containing the personnel files for the Scorpion members. Kyle, Jase...and Liz.

She's not cooperating. Duncan's words chased uneasily through his head. Was it just a ploy to keep Liz's true loyalty secret?

He recalled something Alhasan had said about the Fox's followers being closer than he thought. Before he had time to contemplate the possibility, Sam headed for the door with one final command to his men.

"Tie them up. We need to get out of here now."

Sam addressed Kyle once more. The smug smile on his face told Kyle there was more bad news coming. "The plane is wired with explosives. Once we're airborne we'll blow it, and then when the rest of your team arrives we'll take care of them, as well. Sorry, my friend, I hate for it to end like this. I really did like you."

In the distance, the noise of an approaching chopper tore Sam's attention away.

Jase!

"You're too late," Kyle assured him while trying to sound convincing. "That's Jase and the rest of the Scorpions. You'll never make it out of here alive, Sam. Give yourself up."

"You don't know what you're talking about. They'll be dead soon enough." He turned to his men. "Leave them.

Let's get to the chopper. We need to be airborne to detonate the explosives."

They'll be dead soon enough. What had Sam meant
by that? He had no idea, but the sooner he got everyone
off the plane the better.

She held her side where the knife had ripped her flesh.
Blood soaked her shirt and hand.

Kyle hurried to her. "How bad is it?" he asked with
fear written all over his face.

She tried to be strong. "Not too bad. It's just a flesh
wound. I don't think he nicked anything important." He
didn't believe her, but there was no time to examine the
cut.

"We have to get everyone off now. The second they're
airborne, they'll blow the plane."

Lena faced the couple and younger man. "Are you
hurt or can you walk? We need everyone off the plane
quickly."

Visibly shaken, the couple stared at each other. The
younger man got to his feet. "I'm David, and yes, we can
walk." He took the woman's arm and assisted her while
the older man followed.

"Let me help you." Kyle turned to her and insisted.

She shook her head. "No, I can walk. Take Joseph."

Although Kyle appeared doubtful, he scooped the boy
into his arms. The child fought him. Joseph didn't trust
anyone but her.

Lena stood in front of him and smiled. "Joseph, it's
okay, you can trust him. He's not going to hurt you, I
promise. Come, follow me." She headed for the exit, her
heart pounding with each step. What if they were too

late? She couldn't lose Kyle and Joseph after they'd come through so much.

Once they reached the bottom stair, she saw the chopper slowly rise in the air. "Run for the trees," she yelled, and Kyle grabbed her hand and with Joseph tucked under his arm they raced for the trees nearby.

They'd barely made it to the edge of the woods when the plane went up in a firestorm that knocked them to the ground. The world around her blurred with pain. Bile rose in her throat. She forced in several breaths before it cleared away.

Joseph freed himself from Kyle and ran into her arms, and she flinched.

"It's okay," she struggled to reassure him. "We're safe now. They're not going to hurt us again."

Something in Kyle's expression told her nothing could be farther from the truth.

"What is it?" she asked fearfully.

"He's planning to take out the team once they land. There's only one way to do that. He's got this whole area wired. They'll be waiting for Aaron to land the chopper. We have to stop Sam before he can detonate the rest of the explosives."

Lena slowly got to her feet and headed for the clearing.

"No." Kyle stopped her. "I need you get everyone out of the area in case I can't stop him in time."

She knew what that meant. If he failed, he'd be dead.

She reached for his arm with tears in her eyes. "Please be careful," she whispered. She wanted to say so much more. Tell him that she would love him for the rest of her life, but she didn't have the right to claim his heart any longer.

Please come back to me, she said in her head instead.

He smiled down at her tenderly and his smile held a moment of promise. "I will. Hurry, Lena. Get everyone to safety."

FIFTEEN

Sam's chopper hovered over the wreckage of the plane, waiting for Aaron to land. With the explosion, Aaron had been forced to withdraw from the immediate area. No one on board the Scorpion chopper had any idea Sam was the enemy. They'd think he was assisting.

It was now or never. Kyle had one shot at taking the chopper down. He'd need a direct hit to its engine.

Sam's spotlight panned the area, searching for survivors. They'd open fire the second they spotted him.

The risk was great. Liz and Michael were on board and might possibly die, but he couldn't let Sam detonate those explosives.

Kyle waited until the spotlight was focused on a different area, then he slipped from his coverage and aimed for the engine.

The bullets charged from the Glock. The sound of metal hitting metal followed. Smoke spewed from the chopper's wasted engine and immediately it swayed back and forth. The pilot tried to correct. Without the engine it was useless. The machine slammed into the ground full force.

Aaron brought the chopper closer and homed in on Kyle. Moments later, it kicked up earth as it landed.

After the dust and debris cleared, Kyle headed for the downed machine. As soon as the second chopper was on the ground, Jase and the team rushed to Kyle's aide.

Sam was unconscious in the copilot seat. Kyle felt for a pulse.

"Is he alive?" Jase asked the second he reached the chopper.

"Just barely." Sam's injuries were severe. Several of his men were dead. Those who had survived were in bad shape.

Kyle shoved aside debris until he reached Liz and Michael. They were barely hanging on, as well.

Agent Ryan Samuels climbed through the wreckage until he reached Liz. He was well trained in emergency medicine. Ryan did a quick but thorough exam of both agents. "Liz has a fractured wrist and possibly some broken ribs. Michael may have internal bleeding and he's been stabbed. We need to get them to a hospital right away."

Kyle tried his cell phone again. This time the call went through. The signal blocker must have been inside the plane. He called the local police and briefed them on what was going on.

"What happened here?" Jase asked in disbelief once Kyle had ended the call.

He told his friend the truth about Sam's betrayal.

Jase was clearly in shock. He shook his head in disbelief. "It's unimaginable. Sam was the one we've been searching for all along."

"I know. I still can't believe it, either," Kyle assured him. "Hopefully, with the help of the survivors we'll be able to compile enough evidence to send Sam away for good. And perhaps find out where the weapons are hidden." That was something that concerned him deeply. Where had Sam stashed the weapons?

Jase blew out a breath. "Where's Lena?" he asked when he realized she was nowhere around.

Kyle explained about the explosives. "We need to get everyone out of here as quickly as possible," he said. "It was amazing that the accident didn't detonate them. As soon as the area is cleared, I'll have an explosives team come in and disarm them."

In the distance multiple sirens blared. Help was close.

"Why do you think he took Liz and Michael? And what was he after at headquarters?" Jase asked perplexed by it all.

Kyle only had pieces of the puzzle now. "There's something in the personnel files that he doesn't want us to find, and we need to learn what it is." He hesitated a second and then told Jase his worst fear. "I think someone on our team is working for Sam."

The accusation was as unexpected as it was shocking. "Do you think it could be Liz or Michael? Or both?" Jase asked.

Kyle didn't want to go there. "I don't know. I sure hope not. It could just be more lies. But until we know for sure, we need to search those files carefully."

"You're right." Jase glanced back at the ruined chopper. "Do you think he'll talk?"

Kyle knew who he meant. "Maybe if he believes it will save his life, but I don't believe so." What Sam chose to do didn't matter anymore. All Kyle could think about was Lena. He loved her. But he still had to find a way to forgive her.

* * *

They'd barely made it to the parked car when she witnessed the chopper drop from the sky. Kyle had managed to accomplish a near-impossible feat. She all but forgot about her own injuries. There would be lives at stake. Some from their own team. The Fox. She prayed he was still alive. He needed to be held responsible for his brutality.

Kyle. She was so afraid for him. She knew he wouldn't leave anyone behind, yet each moment he was back there he risked the chance that something would go wrong and the explosives would ignite.

It was hard not to go after him, but she had to think of Joseph. The boy had been clinging to her since she'd carried him from the woods.

She could hear the ambulances coming. She turned in time to see several emergency personnel along with a multitude of cop cars streaming down the road, lights flashing.

Henry was one of the police officers responding. He spotted her and came over. "Heard the commotion on the radio and figured it had something to do with you two. I know I don't have jurisdiction here, but I figured I'd offer my help. Looks like you're worse for the wear. Where are the others?"

She pointed back toward the woods. "They're in there. A chopper went down. There are multiple injuries. They need you. I'll be fine." She told Henry about the explosives.

The chief glanced around at the amount of police officers responding to the call. "You have plenty of help coming. You need to have that wound looked after. You've lost a lot of blood."

Lena finally gave in.

"Who's this young man?" Henry asked curiously.

"He's my friend." She smiled down at the boy who'd stolen her heart.

"You two look a lot alike," he informed her as four more EMTs arrived on the scene. "Come with me." He told them. "We have to hurry. We need to get the wounded out as quickly as possible." Before she had time to process what Henry had said, he was gone.

With Joseph refusing to leave her side, Lena spotted David and Ella's parents, and went over to where they were receiving treatment.

"How are they?" she asked the EMT treating them.

"Surprisingly well considering what they've been through." He got a good look at her and said, "You'd better let me take a look at that wound."

She couldn't imagine how bad she must appear, but she had other priorities. "Can you give us just a minute first?" she asked and the man nodded.

Ella's parents had been through so much, but she needed answers.

She took David aside.

"She's dead, isn't she?" he asked once they were out of earshot and she knew he meant Ella. There was no doubt in her mind that Ella's body had been the one burned beyond recognition.

"Yes. I'm sorry. I know you loved her."

With tears in his eyes he said, "Yes, but to be honest, we haven't seen her in years, so we were pretty certain she was gone." He swallowed back emotion. "Still, it's good to know once and for all." He nodded toward Ella's parents. "It'll be hard for them."

Lena couldn't imagine the pain David and Ella's parents had gone through.

"Can you tell me what happened to you?" she asked.

He glanced over at the elderly couple. They were just recognizable as Ella's parents. They'd lost so much weight and the hardships of prison life had left its toll on their faces.

"We'd barely been there a few weeks when we were attacked. Several people were killed. We were taken prisoner along with Ella. But they separated us pretty quickly," he said and shook his head. "I never saw her again after those first few days."

Sam had planned ahead. Ultimately using Ella's resemblance to Lena to form his deadly plot.

"Thank you for sharing with me. I'll let you get back to them. They're going to need you now more than ever," Lena told him. They'd all have a long road ahead of them.

Lena went over to the EMT who immediately began treating her injury.

She thought about the future. Would she find one with Kyle? She desperately hoped so.

As she had so many times in the past through all those dark years in prison, she'd put her future in God's hands. He hadn't let her down yet. He wouldn't now.

SIXTEEN

When the last of the injured were safely out of the danger zone, Henry sent in the bomb squad to do their job.

Kyle emerged from the woods in time to see the EMT bandaging Lena's side. He couldn't take his eyes off her. He loved her.

"I still can't believe it," Jase mumbled and then rushed to Lena's side. But Kyle couldn't move. If he lived to be a hundred, he didn't think he'd get used to having his wife back.

Jase held her close and Kyle smiled at the reunion. He understood the magnitude of emotions Jase experienced. As he watched, Lena's love for her friend was evident in the tears streaming down her face.

She appeared so lost that his heart melted for her. In his mind one thought became clear. For seven years, he'd prayed for her return. God had granted his prayers. Now it was up to him. He had to forgive her for both their sakes. She'd suffered enough. If he wanted to have a future with her—and he so desperately did—then his bitterness had no place now or ever.

He silently prayed for strength and gave God his anger.

As much as he wanted to find out what Sam was up to, Kyle knew the road ahead for him and Lena would be a rough one. She needed him and he so wanted to be there for her. He'd leave the unraveling of Sam's operation and the possible mole inside the Scorpion team to someone else to uncover. He wanted to save his marriage.

She glanced up at him tentatively. Their gazes held. He loved her more than ever. They had a second chance, and he wasn't going to do anything to jeopardize that. They'd see their baby girl again someday, and perhaps God would bless them with more children in the future.

Lena was holding on to Joseph as if he might disappear from her life. It was then that Kyle realized why he recognized the boy. He had the same dark hair as Lena, and his eyes were gray...just like Kyle's. The realization almost threatened to take his legs from underneath him. Lena believed she'd lost their child.

Alhasan had lied about so many things. Was it possible that Joseph was their son?

She couldn't read anything welcoming in Kyle as he drew near. She struggled to keep the tears away. Had she lost him?

Please, no.

Jase followed her line of sight then hugged her once more. "We have a lot to catch up on and I can't wait for you to meet Reyna, but I think you have other things to sort out right now." He smiled tenderly then stepped away as Kyle drew near. He looked so uncertain that her heart shattered.

"How's she doing?" he asked the EMT.

"She's blessed. A few more inches up and it would have been a different story." He closed his equipment bag and stepped away, and she didn't know what to say. He was better off without her.

"How's the boy?" he asked her and she sensed he wasn't saying what he wanted to. She remembered that trait from the past.

She hugged Joseph close. "He's okay. I won't give him up. He doesn't have anyone, Kyle. I won't give him up," she said with defiance.

The EMT came back with a stuffed bear. "Hey, Joseph, do you think you could help me out? My friend Teddy needs a good home."

The boy stared at the bear in awe. He hadn't had so much as a single toy the entire time he'd been held captive.

"If you could take care of Teddy, it would be a big help for me."

When Joseph hesitated and looked to her, she said, "Go ahead, honey, it's okay. Take it."

Slowly Joseph reached out to take the bear from the man. He stared at it a second longer then clutched it tight.

"Joseph, do you think I could take a look at that wound on your arm?" the EMT asked quietly. "I promise I'll be as gentle as possible."

Joseph cowered closer to Lena's side.

"It's okay. I'll be right over there. I won't be out of your sight for a second."

Slowly the boy released his grasp on her and the EMT showed him all his instruments.

Lena stepped a little away. Her heart was breaking. She had to stay strong. She didn't want Joseph to see her upset.

Admiration flashed in Kyle's eyes. "He loves you so much. He'll need you to move beyond all this." He finally faced her. "Lena, we need to talk."

This was the moment she'd been dreading. She didn't want to hear him say the words.

She couldn't look at him and not fall apart. She stared at Joseph. He was her future.

"Is Sam alive?" she asked, searching for something to say.

"Yes, but he's badly injured," he said quietly.

"What about Liz and Michael? Are they going to make it?" She needed to know those who had tried to save her wouldn't pay with their lives.

"They'll make it. They were very blessed."

It was like they were strangers. The unbearable silence between them was all the proof of the future she needed. "It's okay, you don't have to say it. I know what I did before was…inexcusable. You're better off without me, Kyle. I'm not the person I was before. I don't know if that woman still exists anymore."

When he didn't answer, she knew she had to get away before she broke down. She turned blindly toward Joseph when Kyle caught her hand.

She didn't look at him. "Kyle, please."

He tugged her hand and brought her close, forcing her to look at him.

Kyle cupped her face and the love she thought she'd lost was shining in his eyes. "Babe, I'm so sorry. I gave in to a moment of anger and I had no right to." A sob escaped, but he had her full attention. "I love you, Lena. With all my heart, I love you, and I want to spend the rest of my life with you."

She could barely see much less speak, but it didn't seem to matter. Kyle took her in his arms and kissed her with all his heart, and she returned his kisses with the love she'd almost forgotten existed. Lena held on to him tight, because she was so afraid she'd wake up and realize she was back in the prison.

"I love you, Lena, and I'm so sorry I let you down."

She pulled away and looked into his eyes. "Oh, Kyle," she said in a broken voice. "You didn't let me down. I'm the one who let you down. I hurt you. Because of my foolishness, I lost our child, and I'm so sorry."

He shook his head. "No. You did what you thought was best for everyone in an impossible situation. It wasn't your fault."

She touched his cheek. So happy to be reunited once more. But there was work to be done. "What do you think he was after?" she asked. She of all people needed to know why she and Joseph had paid so dearly.

"I don't know, but there is something in the team's personnel files that he needed. Maybe someone had a connection to Sam that went beyond mere friendship." He shook his head. "Whatever it is, we'll find it, but I'm leaving that for someone else. I just want to be with you and…" He stopped. Kyle stared into her eyes. There was something he wanted to tell her.

"What is it?" she asked, so afraid he'd changed his mind.

"No, it's nothing bad, I promise." He smiled gently at her and then pointed to Joseph. "How old is Joseph again?"

She didn't understand the question. Why was Joseph's age important? "I don't know for sure. Alhasan told me he was around eight years old. Why?"

Kyle shook his head. "I don't buy it. He appears much younger than eight. I'd say he's around six." He waited a second and said, "Lena, have you ever really looked closely at Joseph?"

She turned to do just that. "What do you mean?"

"He has the same hair color as you do. And his eyes…

they're gray like mine." She couldn't speak. She'd never really noticed any of those things until now. She'd just been so in love with the boy.

"Then there's the way you protect him and love him," Kyle continued quietly. "Just like his mother would. Babe, Joseph is our child, I'm almost positive of it. Alhasan lied to you. I noticed the resemblance the second I saw him. It was like there was a bond between us, even though I didn't realize what it was at the time. Joseph is our son, Lena. Our child survived."

She stared at Joseph and finally saw what Kyle did. She'd been so focused through the years on surviving that she hadn't seen the truth that was right there in front of her.

She broke down, tears streaming down her face. "Our child didn't die after all. I—I can't believe it's real."

Joseph must have sensed she was hurting, because he jumped from his perch on the back of the ambulance and ran right into her open arms.

"It's okay, Joseph. It's okay. I'm not crying because I'm sad. I'm crying because I'm just so happy." She hugged him tight. "You're going to come home and live with us. We're going to be a family and we're never going to let anything bad happen to you again."

She was so blessed to have both her husband and the child she thought she'd lost all those years back in her life once more. She had a second chance, and with God's help, she was going to do everything in her power to be worthy of it.

* * * * *

*If you enjoyed this book, don't miss these
other exciting stories from Mary Alford*

*FORGOTTEN PAST
ROCKY MOUNTAIN PURSUIT*

*Find this and other great reads
at www.LoveInspired.com*

Dear Reader,

Can you imagine being held prisoner for more than seven years without remembering anything about your past, your name or if there is someone out there searching for you? It would be so easy to give up. Lose hope. Turn your back on God, even. Yet it is in these dark times that God's love can be felt the strongest. In our weakness, His strength shines like a beacon, guiding us through the difficult moments in our lives.

This is the story behind my latest Love Inspired Suspense, *Deadly Memories*.

Imprisoned for years, Ella Weiss finds herself faced with an impossible situation. Follow through with the deadly plan created by her captors, or lose the child she has grown to love like her own.

After Ella is rescued by Scorpion Agent Kyle Jennings outside a destroyed prison compound in Afghanistan, she must decide if she will take an innocent life to save the child's, or trust Kyle when he tells her he won't let her down.

When we are faced with a difficult situation such as Ella's, we, too, have a choice to make. Trust in our own strength to get us through, or believe God will keep His promises. Letting go of our will and holding on to His can be so hard, but if we have faith in God not to let us down, He'll be there for us just as Kyle was for Ella.

All the best,
Mary Alford

Get 2 Free Books,

Plus 2 Free Gifts—

just for trying the Reader Service!

SPECIAL EXCERPT FROM

*A bounty hunter teams up with an FBI agent to track
down her missing colleague and a killer.*

Read on for an excerpt from Lynette Eason's
BOUNTY HUNTER,
the next book in the exciting new series
CLASSIFIED K-9 UNIT.

A simple twitch of his finger and his sister's killer would
be gone. His two-month quest to find Van Blackman would
be over. Riley Martelli took one more long look at the man
in his sights then lowered the weapon.

He could never kill someone in cold blood. Not even
the man who'd murdered his sister and put his six-year-
old nephew, Asher, in the hospital with a bullet lodged
near his spine.

Van knelt, but Riley couldn't see what he was doing.
Soon, small puffs of smoke drifted from the patch of
ground.

Riley settled the gun back on his shoulder and got a
better look with the scope. Van crouched over the small
flame, pushing the contents as though trying to encourage
a larger blaze. Riley lowered the weapon again.

Now, in a very secluded area of Colorado's Rocky
Mountain National Park, Van moved to stand next to a
black SUV just a few yards ahead of him.

It might be July in Colorado, but it was cold at night, dropping into the forties. Van wore a black ski cap pulled low over his ears, but his height and broad shoulders were harder to disguise. Riley's heart pounded. Finally, he was going to bring his sister's killer to justice. He shifted the rifle on his shoulder for one more look through the scope. He scanned his prey's body.

His target turned and Riley now had a full-on view of his face—and his heart stuttered.

It wasn't Van Blackman.

Disappointment shot through him. He had the wrong man. Riley lowered the rifle with a frustrated sigh. Then frowned and lifted it to stare through the scope once again. The man's face was familiar. Where had he seen him before? Television? Yeah, that was it. Could it be— He focused again.

Yep. That was the missing FBI agent who had been all over the news lately. Morrow was his last name. Jake Morrow. And there was a hundred thousand dollars being offered as a reward for his safe return.

Don't miss
BOUNTY HUNTER by Lynette Eason,
available wherever
Love Inspired® Suspense books and ebooks are sold.

www.LoveInspired.com

LISEXP0617